*THE CAT*

# THE CAT FROM NOWHERE

*ELLIE BLAINE 1920s MYSTERIES*
*BOOK THREE*

# EM BOLTON

EM Bolton asserts the moral right to be identified as the author of this work.
First edition
ISBN:9798871723753

*How could we, why should we say it's the end*
*Is this the one break nothing can mend?*
*When there is so much at stake*
*Why let our hearts ache and ache?*
*All over nothing at all*

**All Over Nothing At All**
**Nora Bayes 1922**

*ELLIE BLAINE 1920s MYSTERIES*

# CHAPTER 1

"OOH, I love this song, Miss Ellie. Ain't it got a lovely melody? My Alfie likes this one, he says, 'cos it's a nice one to slow-dance to. You don't have to watch your feet so much, he says."

Ellie looked up from her letter to watch her maid retracing her practiced dance steps, with her broom standing in for 'her Alfie'. She span elegantly around as the chorus rose, before catching her legs up in the handle and stumbling awkwardly into the writing bureau, tipping over a pen holder and spilling its contents across its surface.

"I hope he dances better than the broom does," Ellie laughed.

Livvy blushed, quickly gathering up scattered pencils. "He does miss. He's very light on his feet, what with all that going up and down ladders he does all day. Very sturdy legs." She blushed again, a deeper red.

"I thought he worked at Mr Titley's butchers?' Ellie said, putting down the letter on a small, walnut-veneered side-table.

"Oh no, miss," Livvy said. "That was Alfie Tanner. I had to end it with him. He had two left feet, he did. Kept treading on my toes. Now I'm seeing Alfie Bowman, what lives over Cowthorpe way and cleans windows. He's a much better dancer. 'Cept now, of course, I don't get a discount on my lamb chops no more."

Ellie shook her head gently. "Well, I'm sure he's worth it."

"Oh, he is, miss," Livvy said, stepping back to survey the table to make sure she'd put everything back in place, then carefully straightening out a crooked writing pad. "He's a proper gentleman, is my Alfie."

"I should hope he is," Ellie said, with mock-seriousness.

"And he knows all about the latest music and what-not, he does. He's a right 'cool cat', ain't that what you say in America, miss?"

"I guess so," Ellie said, raising a sharp eyebrow. "A bit like Mr Madison there, he's a pretty cool cat too, and he seems to like this song." She nodded towards the fat ginger cat who belonged to housekeeper Mrs Madison and who was currently swinging his head rapidly from side-tot- side to keep pace with the edge of the record turning on the gramophone.

"Shoo, shoo!" Livvy Turpin said, wafting her fingers towards the cat to chase him off before he decided it was the right time to jump on his 'prey'. "Don't you go messin' about with Miss Ellie's music now."

"What's this one called?" Ellie said, nodding towards the spinning disc that had caught Mr Madison's eye.

"All By Myself, miss," Livvy said. "Nice, innit?"

Ellie shrugged. "It's got a sweet melody, alright," she said. "I usually prefer something a bit more lively, though."

"Did Lord Melmersby… Mr Richard…" Livvy corrected herself to the less formal name Ellie preferred, "is that one of his?"

Ellie nodded. Getting hold of a gramophone record was no easy task in rural Yorkshire, and Richard had been kind enough to bring some of the latest songs Ellie had asked for, on his trips back to Melmersby from London. He'd been a more regular visitor over the last few months, particularly since his friend Dr Charles Waterman had to take time off to visit his sick mother, and Richard had stepped in to cover his practice. She preferred the ragtime and jazz music she listened to back in Indiana, but he would occasionally drop off one or two he'd picked himself; not always matching her taste, Ellie thought, although she would never tell him that.

She picked up the letter again that she'd been reading when Livvy waltzed in, and read it back to herself.

> *Hello old bean, hope all is spiffy with you in Melmersby and it's not too dreadfully dull having no ghastly murders to solve any more. I have the most terrific news to tell you. Yours Truly has now officially been installed as a barrister! Yes, dear thing, I am now a lady of the law. Of course I wasn't the first, which is an awful bore, but the lady who pipped me to the post is a frightfully good sort and I might almost say she deserved it, if I was the kind of person to be so gracious, which of course you know I'm not, but you shan't breathe a word of that.*
>
> *Anyway, I shall say no more in writing and instead absolutely insist you come at your earliest convenience to London to celebrate with me and some of my chums in the big city. And of course, by your convenience I mean I expect you here a week on Thursday on the dot and shall not take no for an answer.*
>
> *Toodle pip!*
>
> *Your dearest friend, Georgie*

Ellie smiled to herself. As usual, Georgie was giving her no choice but she was happy to go along with her plans. She'd not seen her friend since she left for London just after the new year, and six months was far too long to go without the sort of adventures they usually found themselves in. Though she hoped any excitement might be confined to nightclubs, museums and shopping rather than the sort of scrapes they had got themselves into in Yorkshire the previous year.

She looked at the pile of other letters on the side table by her chair. Other demands, none as friendly or as welcome as Georgie's: bills, requests from tenants of the estate lands, bank letters, building surveys and countless official documents. She'd not fully understood the value, or the responsibility, of Richard's gift to her until it came to getting a valuation to renew the insurance for the house and its contents. 'Far too much', Ellie had told him, but he insisted Melmersby Hall was as he presented it, an inheritance from his brother, the man she should have married but for the war, rather than a gift on his part. All the same, she still felt a little guilt, and more than a little apprehension, at the size of the bequest she had taken on.

"You off to London then?" Livvy said, leaning over Ellie's shoulder. "Not that I was reading what Miss Georgina wrote or nothing," she said, urgently picking up her duster and finding a convenient web that needed brushing away from the window sill to her side.

Ellie folded the letter again. "It sure looks like it." she said. "Do you know anywhere you think I should visit?"

Livvy scratched at her chin. "Well, I ain't never been, miss. Not that I wouldn't love to, but no-one's ever taken me there and I shouldn't like to go to the big city on my own. I've heard it's full of all sorts of villains and such. Mind you, I should like to go dancing at one of them fancy dance halls they have there. My Alfie says they have all the best bands from all over, miss. Even from America, if you can believe it."

Ellie wondered if there really could be more villains there than she'd met so far in her time in Yorkshire, and hoped, for the sake of her visit, that she didn't run into any of them if there were. "Perhaps your Alfie might be able to tell me if there are any good shows on when I'm there?"

Livvy shrugged. "He said somethin' about it, miss. He reads all the music news you see, in the papers and whatnot. Now I come to think about it, there's supposed to be this famous jazz band coming over from America this month, he told me. 'Course, he wanted to take me to London to see them, but I told him, I said: 'Alfie Bowman, I is not waltzing off to London with you without we have a chaperone, so don't you get any ideas'. That's what I told him."

Ellie sat up. "You'd be more than welcome to come with me."

Livvy shook her head, along with her duster. "That is very kind of you, Miss Ellie, but I 'as promised to go with my old mum to Scarborough for her six-monthly constitutional that week– Brix Riley's Blue Notes!"

"I'm sorry?" Ellie said. "Brix who?"

"Brix Riley's Blue Notes," Livvy said, nodding to herself to confirm how pleased she was with herself for remembering. "That's the American jazz band. You heard of them?"

Ellie shook her head. "No, are they new?"

"I don't know too much about 'em, miss," Livvy said. "'Cept my Alfie, he said, they've got this new saxophone player what everyone says is the bee's knees, miss. Had a very strange name, he did. Now what was it? Oh yes, The Cat from Nowhere, they call him, that's what my Alfie said."

"Cat from Nowhere?"

"Aye miss," Livvy said, suddenly sitting down on the arm of the wing-back chair opposite Ellie, as if she had a story to tell that demanded her full attention. "My Alfie was itching to see him play – reckons he's supposed to be the best in the world, that's what folk are saying anyhow. But he's a man of mystery, so they say."

"What kind of mystery?" Ellie said, sitting forward, suddenly intrigued.

"Well, apparently he just appeared one day. Just like that. No one never heard of him before or nothing, just appeared."

"Appeared? Out of thin air?"

"Aye – well, Alfie says he read how he just turned up one night, at a show the band was doing, and the next thing you know he's in the band. No one ever heard of him before, or nothing – just appeared from nowhere and the next minute he's playing with the hottest band in America. Supposed to be the best there is too, miss, that's what my Alfie says."

Ellie raised an eyebrow. "Well, sounds like a good story to sell tickets. But if this…"

"Cat from Nowhere, miss," Livvy finished for her.

Ellie nodded. "If he's as good as you say, maybe I'll see if Georgie fancies a little night of jazz when we're in London."

# CHAPTER 2

GEORGIE'S letter had been surprisingly short and to the point for her, Ellie thought, but she was more than making up for it now at her elegant apartment in London's fashionable Grosvenor Square.

"And then," she said, waving her cocktail stick around like a cavalry saber, "out of the fog stepped half a dozen bobbies, and the dashing Lord Melmersby. Well you should have seen that dastardly rogue's face. He ran off like a startled whippet, straight into the bog. They had to haul him out and march him off in cuffs. It was quite the adventure."

"It was quite the scandal," one of Georgie's friends, a tall, elegant woman who'd been introduced to Ellie simply as Sarah, said. "I read all about the whole affair in The Times. We were all terribly excited to finally get to meet the daring detective."

Sarah beamed widely at Ellie, who gave a slightly embarrassed nod over the top of her martini in return. Sarah had insisted on hearing the tales of her detective work almost as soon as she walked through the door, but by the way she finished most of Georgie's anecdotes for her, she suspected she had already heard them many times before.

"So what is it you do? Do you work with Georgie?" Ellie said, hoping to move the conversation on from herself.

"Oh no," Sarah said, batting a dismissive hand. "I'm afraid I should make the most terrible lawyer, I don't have Georgie's patience for dusty old books, and even dustier old men. And besides, I should look simply terrible in a powdered wig. I am, I suppose, what you might call a 'lady of leisure', though, frankly, that is far harder work than one might imagine it to be."

"Sarah was married to a fabulously wealthy shipping magnate," Georgie said, smiling slyly at her friend. "And now she is a fabulously wealthy divorcee."

Sarah nodded firmly. "A man of impeccable taste and style," she said. "Except when it came to the 'ladies' he liked to spend his leisure time with. In that, he was very frugal and always seemed to go for the cheapest."

Ellie shook her head. "I'm sorry to hear that."

Sarah waved away her concern theatrically. "Oh, don't be, darling. He is paying very dearly for it now, and I am doing my best to spend his money with considerably more enthusiasm than it is offered."

Sarah certainly didn't seem to be suffering too much from her situation, Ellie thought. She was dressed from head to toe in what she imagined must be the very latest fashion in London, and her fingers and neck sparkled with bright, and very expensive-looking, stones. If this is how she dressed for a visit to her friend's apartment, Ellie wondered what she might look like on a night on the town. She certainly carried it well: high cheekbones and jet black hair framing striking blue eyes. Ellie imagined she wouldn't find it too hard to find another millionaire if she decided single life was no longer for her.

Georgie's other friend there, Liz, was a little more down-to-earth, dressed in a sober tweed jacket and ankle-length skirt and wearing a pair of thick-rimmed tortoiseshell glasses. She, Ellie had already learned, did work with Georgie, or at least had trained in law with her. Liz might not have had Sarah's outer confidence, but she certainly didn't appear to lack any belief in herself.

"Now I can't promise you murder and mayhem here in London," Liz said, leaning across Georgie to talk to Ellie. "Though, heaven knows, we have enough of it, though not in the places we frequent

I'm pleased to say. But if you want to make the most of your time in the big city, you have done well to talk to Sarah and I. Georgie, old thing, we love you to bits but… well, you can take the girl out of the country but you can't take the country out of the girl. We shall make sure to show your pal Ellie the very best spots in town."

Georgie did her best to hide her disgruntlement at her friend's comments, though not very well, Ellie thought. "Well, I might not be born within the sound of Bow Bells," she said, "but I do like to think that I know my way around London, and I know a few places we simply must visit. I was thinking we could–"

"Tomorrow," Liz cut in, "we shall take you for afternoon tea at the Café Royal, but first we must go to Oxford Street to pick out some clothes for you. I'm sure you are quite the dandy in Yorkshire, but we are in London now and so we will need to spin up a little capital stardust for you."

Ellie forced an awkward smile. She wasn't sure she was a 'dandy' anywhere, or that she really wanted to be. She glanced at Georgie, her expression enough to let her friend know she wouldn't mind a little back-up here.

"Nonsense!" Georgie said, subtly nudging her way back past Liz to face Ellie and rest her hand on her shoulder. "Ellie is quite fashionable enough as it is." Ellie wasn't convinced her friend's face portrayed the same belief as her words, but she was glad of the support nonetheless. "Now, didn't you say you wanted to catch a little live entertainment while you were here? Some jazz or such?"

Georgie's musical taste - despite her unfortunate brush with contemporary music at Lady Danver's ball - was firmly set at the more high-brow end of the scale, so the fact she wasn't suggesting a night at the opera told Ellie that her friend definitely had her back here. "I heard there was an American jazz band in town?" Ellie said. "I'd definitely like to see that if we can."

"Oh, I love a bit of jazzmattaz!" Sarah said excitedly. "We shall be sure to do that. I shall find my most outrageous flapper dress and we shall be thoroughly decadent."

Liz clapped her hands in agreement, although her smile looked a little forced. "That sounds like a splendid idea," she said. "I shall arrange tickets to the Criterion, I know a fellow who—"

Sarah's loud tutting stopped Liz in her tracks. "Forget the Criterion, that's yesterday's news. We shall go to the Starlight Club. Ellie said she wanted American jazz, and they have the Tommy Marvin Band, all the way from Chicago, it's quite the thing, so I'm told."

Liz's expression darkened, but she kept her bright smile in place. "Well, if you wanted American jazz, I should think the Blue Parakeet would be the place. Though of course, one really has to be someone to get in there on Saturday night. They say it's the hottest ticket in town. Oh, unless of course you know someone, Sarah?"

Sarah shook her head, her expression exactly as Ellie imagined Liz intended it to look.

Georgie coughed. "Well, as it happens, I do know someone."

"Really?" Liz said, frowning.

"Yes," Georgie said. "Really. Even a country bumpkin like me does have the odd connection up her smock sleeve."

Liz and Sarah hurried to let Georgie know they didn't think she was a country bumpkin at all, and Georgie batted away their protests with as much sincerity as they were offered.

"The most exciting show in town, by all accounts," she said to Ellie. "Can't get a ticket for love nor money, they sell out as soon as they release them. Luckily I happen to know that one can get some in return for previously having helped the owner with, shall we say, a little legal matter. We shall go over to the club for a late lunch and all will be arranged."

"That sounds marvellous," Sarah said, sincerity back in her voice at the prospect. "Will Richard be there?"

"You know Richard?" Ellie said.

Sarah shrugged. "Never met the fellow, but I like what I hear about him. I should like to be introduced – oh, as long as I'm not stepping where I shouldn't?"

Ellie looked around before realising Sarah was talking about her. She shook her head. "No, not at all."

"Jolly good," Sarah said with a waft of her hand. "I shouldn't wish to tread on anyone's toes on the dancefloor, so to speak."

"Richard isn't much of a dancer," Georgie said dryly.

"Oh, darling," Sarah said with a subtle smile, "I'm sure that's only because he hasn't met the right dance partner."

# CHAPTER 3

"AH, Lord Melmersby. Richard. Shall I call you Richard? Delighted to meet you, Richard, you are just as I imagined you." Sarah hadn't waited for Richard to stand from his seat at the club table before offering her hand, which he took with a cautious smile.

"Do I know you?" he said, frowning.

"Sarah Fotheringay," she said. "Of course, that's my married name, but I have kept it, rather like the diamonds. They both suit me, don't you think?"

"Delighted to meet you," Richard said, only slightly easing his frown.

"And I am Elizabeth Strummond," Liz said, quickly offering her hand. "You can call me Liz, though. Everyone does."

Richard nodded, then pulled out the seats from around the table to offer them to the newcomers. The table they sat at was the only occupied one in the room, the others covered with upturned chairs, and the rest of the club empty but for a man sitting alone at the bar, and two others busying themselves with setting up the dark stage at the far side of the room.

"Good to see you again, Richard," Ellie said, smiling as she took her seat.

"You too," Richard said, looking suddenly more relaxed. "I trust all is still going well at Melmersby Hall?"

Ellie nodded. "Same as always, you know how it is."

Richard smiled again, in a way that suggested he knew exactly how it usually was. "Oh, I'm terribly sorry," he said. "I should have introduced you to my new acquaintance here. Georgie, you already know him I believe, but this is Mr Alan Maguire."

The large, heavy-set man half-stood to nod his head around the table. "Ladies. Call me Al," he said in a broad, East London accent. "Welcome to the Blue Parakeet. It's not much, but it's mine. I 'ave to say you've picked a great time to visit, these boys I 'ave on tonight are the best of the best, all the way from Chicago."

"Brix Riley's Blue Notes," Richard said, with a tone that suggested he was well acquainted with the band, although Ellie was sure he'd have only learned that name a few minutes before they arrived.

"Brix Riley," Al beamed, "featuring the new jazz sensation Louis Luther – the man they call The Cat from Nowhere, and boy can that cat play!" Al whistled sharply, pulling up the lapels of his velvet-trimmed jacket.

"The Cat from Nowhere?" Georgie said. "He's not actually a cat is he? Only there's this ginger beast at Melmersby that everyone always assumes is a man before they meet him, so perhaps…."

Al looked to Richard for clarity, and he simply shrugged.

"No," Al said, "he's not a cat, but when you hear him blow you might think he's a songbird – you ain't heard nothing like him."

"Why is he called the Cat from Nowhere?" Liz said, sipping at the small cup of espresso that a waiter had just put in front of her.

"Well," Al said, 'because he's a swinging cat on the sax–"

"And he's from nowhere?" Georgie said.

Al looked at her again as if he wasn't sure how serious she was being. "In a kind of way, yes," he said. "Hey, why don't I get the big man to tell you. Brix! Come and meet some friends of mine."

Al had hollered over to the 'big man' - the short, thin, wiry figure in a loose-fitting grey jacket who had been propping up the empty bar across the dancefloor from them. Ellie imagined he must have got that title from his standing as band leader, rather than his physical stature. The man gave a slight nod as he walked over, pulling a chair from another of the tables to turn backwards, dropping down to straddle it like a saddle and face the table.

"Ladies and gentlemen," Al said, "the finest band leader in jazz, Mr Brix Riley."

Brix gave what barely passed for a smile. He had a face that made Ellie think of one of the hungry alley dogs that hung around outside her backyard in Indianapolis; the same street-wise fierceness that told you it might be best to keep your distance.

"They were just asking about The Cat," Al said. "Thought I'd let you tell them."

Brix pulled a toothpick from his jacket pocket, turning it several times in his hand before popping it into his mouth and chewing at it. "The Cat? Best I've ever played with," he said, his voice as rough as a hard-gravel road. "And I've played with the best. That's about as much as I can tell you, cos it's about as much as anyone knows."

"Tell him how he joined the band," Al said, smiling nervously, as if he was worried the story wouldn't live up to the billing.

Brix took the toothpick out of his mouth, jabbing it in the direction of the stage where the band's instruments were set up for that night's performance. "We were in a club in Chicago, little bit like this one here," he said. "Two years ago this Fall. Fifth night of a three-week residency. Just played our first set, like always. Band was swinging, like always. Not two songs in, playing hot on a little blues number by Clarence Williams. Clay was laying down a heavy beat–"

"Parry Clayton," Al said. "Great bass player."

Brix glared at him and Al looked down at the table.

"Clay was playing some swinging lines, all set up for Tommy to blow–"

"Tommy Marvin," Al whispered, then held up an apologetic hand to let Brix continue.

"Like I say," Brix growled, "Tommy's all set to play his solo, then out of nowhere this cat steps up from his seat at the back of the room, and I see he's got a saxophone in his hand. Well, Tommy just stands there, not sure what this guy is playing at, then the cat starts to blow. He just dropped right in, uninvited. For two bars I was ready to get up and kick his jumped up…behind, 'scuse me ladies… kick him out the door. But by the third bar, well I knew. He was the real thing. Ain't heard nothin' like it, and nor do I expect to again 'till I'm through them pearly gates and swinging with the angels."

"So you asked him to join the band?" Ellie said.

"I didn't ask, I told him," Brix said. "If Brix tells you to play in his band, you play. I called out to him, across the floor. I said: 'boy, what's your name,' and he says its Louis Luther. And I say 'well, Louis Luther, you are now in the Blue Notes'."

"How did Tommy feel about that?" Liz said.

Brix fixed her with a hard stare. "I didn't stop to ask him. I only need one saxophone in my band,

and I only want the best. Tommy weren't the best no more, so I didn't have to tell him where he stood."

"He left?" Ellie said.

"Left, got replaced; same difference. Louis stepped up on the stage, Tommy stepped off. Didn't see him again, 'cept to give him his last paycheck."

"Right there? That same night?" Georgie said incredulously. "You just replaced him in the middle of a show?"

"Now, miss…?"

"Georgie."

"Miss Georgie. If you had a penny right there in your hand, and I was to say to you how would you like to swap that penny right this minute for a hundred dollar bill. I don't suppose you'd take too much time to think about the what fors and the whys of it, you'd take that hundred dollars right out of my hand, and I don't suppose you'd care too much, either, for what became of your penny. That's how it was."

Al grinned again, still looking nervously at Brix. "Old Tommy's done alright," he said. "He's got his own band now, doing very well. In fact they're playing across town this week. Two American bands at the same time, quite the swinging time in old London town."

"Is that the Tommy Marvin band you mentioned, Sarah?" Ellie said

"It is, absolutely," Sarah said. "I hear they are rather well thought of."

Brix shrugged. "Sure, Tommy is a fine player. One of the best. Just not the best."

"They're playing at the Starlight Club," Al said. "Run by a good friend of mine, Spats Corliss. Well, a friendly rival, let's say. I suspect his dander was put up when I bagged Brix and the boys so he's tried to go one-up on me by bringing Tommy Marvin in the week before my show starts. If he was hoping that would affect my ticket sales he's in for a bit of a let-down. I'm afraid I am doing very well, yes very well indeed. You boys are an absolute hit!" He beamed at Brix, who didn't return the smile.

Sarah took the cue to lean in and take Al's hands firmly in hers, smiling sweetly. "Yes, we heard tickets for your show were like gold-dust. It would be absolutely marvellous if we could get our hands on some. I don't suppose you could squeeze a few little ones in for the opening night, could you, Al darling?"

Al coloured slightly. "Sorry sweetheart," he said. "I've had to turn away some of the biggest names in London, I'd get myself in a whole heap of trouble if I let anyone else in tonight. But I told Georgie here I can get you tickets for tomorrow night. I can just about fit another table in if I move things around. It won't be the best spot, I'm afraid, but how does that sound?"

Sarah shrugged and released her grip, her expression suggesting to Ellie that she wasn't used to not getting exactly what she asked for. "Yes, well, I suppose that's decent of you."

Richard, who had been sitting in silent thought while Al spoke, suddenly sat up. "Mr Riley," he said, "I was wondering—"

"Only my accountant calls me Mr Riley, and that's only because I keep him in fine cigars," Brix said, pushing his chair forward an inch. "Call me Brix."

"Brix," Richard said as formally as he could, "I wonder how the devil anyone can tell how good a chap is as a musician after just a few notes. Wasn't it something of a risk to shoo off your original fellow without seeing what the other chap could really do?"

Brix smiled for the first time. "Well sir, it would be a risk for most, but they don't have Brix Riley's ears. You see, every player has a voice, and its as unique as a fingerprint – ain't no one's voice the same as anyone else's. And I can know a musician – know everything about him – just from hearing that voice. It's in the way they play, the way they breathe, the way they squeeze their soul right through those brass pipes. You can't buy it, you can't change it, you can't train it; it's who you are and who you will always be. Just a handful of the very best have a good voice, like Tommy; most have a terrible voice, even those who do this for a living. But then every once in a very blue moon, someone has a great voice. A truly great voice. Louis has a great voice. Best I've ever heard."

Ellie looked over Brix's shoulder to where three men had now stepped onto the stage at the back of the room. Brix stood up, nodding silently to the table then shuffling over to join the men.

"Now, I'm sorry I couldn't get you in tonight," Al said, "but hopefully this will make up for it. It looks like the boys are just having a quick run through a couple of numbers, it's your lucky day."

Sarah and Liz, who had their backs to the stage, now turned their chairs around to watch the men as they set themselves in their places. A small, nervous looking, man with close-cropped strawberry-blond hair, set himself down on the drum stool, fidgeting with the cymbals to get them in just the right place. To the left of him, a tall, broad-shouldered man was carefully tuning an upright bass, while the third man — wiry and intense-looking, immaculately dressed in a black suit and white-trimmed fedora — stood silently staring at the floor, saxophone in hand.

"Is that The Cat?" Liz said, nodding at the well-dressed man.

"It is," Al said, beaming. "Wait 'till you hear him."

Brix nodded to the men, then picked up a clarinet from a stand at the front of the stage. "Sheikh of Araby," he said firmly. "Ben, count us in."

The nervous-looking man behind the drums hit a count on his sticks and the band started to swing, Brix taking up the melody while the bass kept a driving rhythm. The Cat still stared at the floor, unmoving, as if he was in another place.

"They're rather good, aren't they?" Sarah said, clapping her hands together in time to the beat.

"I suppose," Georgie said, shrugging. "It's hardly Tosca, but I can't deny they have a certain style."

Brix finished a long flourish on the clarinet, then nodded to the Cat, who lifted up his head coolly and brought a battered and worn-looking saxophone to his lips to blow.

"Stop. Stop! Stop!" Brix yelled suddenly. The Cat glared at him, putting down his saxophone again and returning his gaze to the floor. "Ben, hold on there a minute," he said, nodding at the drummer who Ellie thought looked more nervous than ever.

Brix stepped down from the small platform he stood on to play, fiddling with his wrist, then held out his hand to the drummer. "I've got a present for you Ben, do you want it?"

The drummer shook his head, now looking positively petrified.

"You sure?" Brix said. "It's a nice watch. A Hamilton. I thought you could make use of it."

"Hey Brix—" the bass player started.

Brix ignored him. "It's got 17 jewels, runs smooth as buttered ice. And you know what I like best about it? It keeps great time. So I was just asking myself, how come a watch that only cost me forty bucks keeps such great time, but a guy who costs me twice that a month can't even decide if he should go too fast or too slow?"

"Brix, I–" the drummer started.

Brix hurled the watch at him, the drummer ducking at the last second to avoid it hitting him full on the head.

"Whoa! Would you look at that!" Brix said, turning round to the rest of the band. "Little Ben's timing is just fine when he's looking after himself." He turned back to the man, who was now half-cowering behind his kit. "Were you dragging or pushing the beat then? Cos I couldn't work out which one you were doing. You hit everything but the beat. How about you try to miss the beat next time, chances are you'd get it right if you were trying to get it wrong."

Ben sat up again, holding up his hands in apology. "I'm sorry Brix, let's just–"

"This ain't some provincial vaudeville act, boy!" Brix snarled. "It's my band, with my name on it, and my reputation. And if you play like that tonight, so help me, I will walk across this stage and haul you out of that seat of yours and put my goddamn watch in your place. At least it ticks in time."

Ben said nothing, but nodded to the rest of the band to start the count again.

Ellie shook her head. "Is he always like that?" she asked Al.

Al hunched up his shoulders. "I guess that's what it takes to be the best?"

"Why doesn't he just get another drummer, if he doesn't like him?" Georgie asked, looking sympathetically at Ben, who was watching Brix carefully as he played. "He was quick enough to get rid of Tommy Marvin."

Al held out his hands. "Ben's father owns the record company," he said. "It would cost too much to get rid of him, and the only thing Brix values more than making great music is making great money."

"I think I've probably seen enough," Ellie said, pulling back her chair. "I'd rather wait to hear them when there's a full house. Are you coming, Georgie?"

Georgie turned her head back from where she was watching the band. "What? Oh, yes. What about you girls? Richard?"

Liz and Sarah shook their heads, still transfixed by the band who were back in full swing.

"I'll stay a little while," Richard said. "I need to pop into the surgery this afternoon, so I shall stay around here, it's just a short cab ride away."

Ellie smiled and raised her hand to say goodbye, doing the same to Al with a nod of thanks for his hospitality.

"See you girls tomorrow night," Al called after them. "Just you wait – it's going to be a hell of a show!"

# CHAPTER 4

"WELL I thought he was simply beastly!" Liz said, passing the sugar tongs to Georgie while vigorously stirring her own cup. "I've half a mind not to go to the show tonight."

"Oh, he ain't too bad once you get to know him. Well he is, but I guess we're all used to it now." Parry Clayton pushed aside his empty plate to show he'd had enough to eat, after the sixth of the macarons Georgie insisted he tried.

"That poor drummer," Georgie said. "If that had been me I would have taken that watch and put it somewhere so Brix would tick every time he sat down."

Ellie laughed. "I don't think even Brix would be brave enough to throw a watch at you, Georgie."

She lifted the tea-pot to offer another cup to Clay, but he shook his head.

"It sure was nice of you girls to invite me along," he said, looking around the opulent surroundings of the Cafe Royal tea room. "I ain't never been in a place as fancy as this before. Fact I don't think they even have places as fancy as this back home."

Ellie wasn't sure they had places as fancy as this anywhere. The mirrored walls and painted ceiling were entwined with extravagant plasterwork, dripping with beautifully applied gold-leaf; the whole room was softly perfumed by the perfectly-set flower arrangements and the enticing scent of freshly-baked patisserie. She had almost thought she was getting used to the grandeur of English high society after nearly 18 months at Melmersby Hall, but now it felt like she had stepped into another world altogether.

"Oh, it's our absolute pleasure," Liz said, taking hold of Clay's hand across the table. "If you are going to entertain us it is only right we entertain you."

Liz and Sarah had made a point of meeting the band after the rehearsal, and a bigger point of inviting them all, bar Brix, to join them for afternoon tea ahead of the second night's show. Only Parry 'Clay' Clayton had taken them up on the offer, but that didn't seem to have dampened Liz's delight at rubbing shoulders with the hottest jazz band in town.

"I shall come to the show, of course," she said. "Despite the manners of that… Brix. But I shall simply refuse to applaud any of his playing."

"Why do you stick with him, if he treats you all so badly?" Ellie said. "I imagine Louis would be in demand anywhere, and I'm sure you'd have no trouble finding a band who wanted you too."

Clay shrugged. "Brix is the best," he said. "He knows jazz like no-one else. Besides, he pays better than anyone else. I love the blues, but I'm pretty taken with the green too, if you know what I mean. But there's other reasons too, especially for men like me and The Cat."

"Such as?" Georgie said, swallowing a mouthful of choux pastry bun.

Clay paused for a moment, putting down his fork before answering. "Folks like us, where we come from – well, we don't always have the same choices as other folks do. Brix, now he might be 'ornery as an old yard dog, but he don't care nothin' about a man 'cept how he plays. Black, white, polkadot – it's all the same to him; as long as you play good, ain't nothin' else matters. And if you play good, he don't give you no trouble."

"Hmm," Liz muttered. "Well, be that as it may, I still don't like him."

Clay smiled. "Most folks don't, miss, and I expect that's just how he likes it. Brix only cares how people think he plays, and how he puts a band together. He don't fuss too much on nothin' else at all."

"Well, I don't know much about jazz," Georgie said. "But from what I heard yesterday I suppose he does do that rather well, at least."

"He sure does, miss, he sure does." Clay looked down at the small pocket watch attached to his pin-striped waistcoat and shook his head. "Now I'm real sorry, but if you'll excuse me, I better be getting back and getting ready for the show, 'cos I'm going to have to play just as well tonight if you don't want to see him throwing a watch at me." He smiled broadly as he stood, nodding to the women around the table as he turned to leave.

"Clay, mate – do you have a minute?" As he had stood, a ruddy-faced, thin, red-haired man, who had been dining alone at a neighbouring table while they ate, stood as well and now stepped across to put his hand out to introduce himself. "Eric Prendergast, London Evening Post. I was just wondering if I might be able to grab a quick word with you?"

Clay took the man's hand cautiously. "Sorry, sir, I was just—"

"I'm writing a piece about the Battle of the Blues – your lot and Tommy Marvin in town at the same time. Exciting times for all of us music lovers here in old London. It'd be great to get a quote from you, Mr Clayton. What do you make of the big rivalry? The showdown between Tommy and The Cat from Nowhere. Bit of a grudge match, right?"

Clay shook his head and took a deep breath. "Now Mr…"

"Prendergast," the reporter confirmed.

"Mr Prendergast," Clay said, putting his hands on his hips and looking down at the man, who stood a good head shorter than him. "I know jazz is a pretty new thing on the scene here, but I'm sure it works just the same as it does back home. It sounds to me like you're writing for the sports pages, so maybe you could introduce me to your jazz guy and I'll see if I have something to say to him."

The reporter shook his head. "I am the 'jazz guy', I was just wondering–"

"There ain't no 'grudge match'," Clay said, firm but calm. "You can quote me on that. Tommy is a friend, to all of us, and we're all here to play music and keep good folk entertained. Ain't no showdown, ain't no battle."

The man cleared his throat. "There is as far as the readers of the London Evening Post are concerned. And if you pick up a copy tonight, you'll see who won. I caught you fellas last night, and Tommy the night before. Just writing up my piece now for this evening's edition. You can read all about it later."

Clay frowned. "I'll be busy playing later, Mr Prendergast of the London Evening Post. Maybe I'll get hungry after the show, and you can wrap up some of your famous fish and chips for me with that paper of yours."

"I like it," Eric Prendergast said, turning to Ellie with a sly grin. "Sense of humour. I like that in a performer." He turned back to pat Clay on the arm. "I'll drop off a copy for you, hopefully my piece won't spoil your appetite."

Clay turned back to the table, ignoring the reporter. "Enjoy the show tonight, ladies. I'll see you later."

"Oh, one more thing," Eric called after Clay as he walked towards the door. "I've been trying to get an interview with The Cat. Could you remind him; he hasn't responded to any of my messages. I would think he'd be keen to talk to me, we've got a lot to talk about."

Clay shook his head and continued out of the door, holding up his hand up to the table as he left.

* * *

The Blue Parakeet was as busy as Ellie had expected. The club's small, gloss-black door was lit by the gaudy blue and red of an odd-looking neon bird that hung over it, throwing its flickering light onto the front of a queue that had formed alongside the club's paint-peeling walls, and round into a narrower alley that ran behind. Along the line of fashionably-dressed punters – some of the men in sharp, double-breasted suits and women in loose-fitting, calf-length dresses – there was an excited air of anticipation. A few had clearly already been enjoying the hospitality of the numerous Soho bars nearby and there was a little jostling for places along the line, some of it good-natured, and some not so much.

Georgie looked along the slow-moving line, hands on hips, and shook her head. "No, this won't do," she said. "The show will have started before we even get it. I am calling in a favour. Wait there."

She marched towards the door and Ellie looked quizzically at Richard, who shrugged in return as Georgie began an animated conversation with the large, lantern-jawed doorman. Whatever she was saying, it was obviously important enough to get him to send his smaller companion back into the club carrying her message.

"Georgie never ceases to impress me," Richard said, smiling. "I should hate to be the poor lawyer who has to stand against her when she finally gets into court."

"She's definitely got the power of persuasion," Ellie said. "When she says she doesn't take no for an answer she really means it."

The night was warm and windless, and the narrow street hung with the expensive scent of perfume and cigar smoke. Ellie turned her head as the sound of music now caught the night air. At first she thought it was coming from inside the club, but the sound was too clear, and it was calling her attention away from the open door and towards where the queue turned into the alleyway. Under a flickering corner street light, she could see a man – shabbily dressed and shoeless – sitting on a small wooden box while he played a saxophone that looked almost as battered as he did. The sound – raspy and harsh at times on the worn out instrument – didn't detract from the effortless flow and sweet melody that the man conjured from it. A young man from the queue leaned out to toss a small coin into the hat at the man's feet, and he stopped playing just long enough to say a word of thanks. Most of the queue, though, ignored him; chatting, laughing or arguing amongst themselves as they shuffled forwards past him and towards the doors of the Blue Parakeet.

Ellie was so caught up in the playing that she didn't notice Georgie return from her negotiation with the door staff. Her friend gave a sharp cough and Ellie turned to see her gesturing the way to the door, where Al Maguire now stood, calling them in with a wave of his hand.

"I told you he owed me a favour," Georgie said through the side of her mouth, as she escorted Richard and Ellie past the disgruntled glares at the front of the queue and in through the neon-lit door of the club.

"Thank you Mr Maguire," Richard said, raising his hat as the club-owner stepped back to let him pass.

"No problem, sir," he said. "Always happy to help a friend in need." Al nodded at Georgie, who returned the gesture.

Ellie stopped, her eyes adjusting to the bright lighting of the entrance corridor but her ears still fixed on the sound of the street musician.

"Who's the guy with the sax?" Ellie said, glancing back out of the door as she spoke to Al.

"Him?" Al said, stretching his thick neck slightly to look out into the street. "That's old Jacques, looking for his drinking money. He's practically part of the furniture in this street; been 'ere longer than the club. He's alright."

Ellie moved in closer to the wall of the entrance lobby as a short man and his taller partner jostled their way through the door and past her. "He's very good," Ellie said.

Al shrugged. "He's not too shabby."

I would have thought he could play professionally," she said. "I mean, not just for tips on the street."

Al shook his head. "Just goes to show you, Miss Ellie, what a narrow and winding path we showmen have chosen. It's not enough just to be good, you've got to be smart too, one step ahead. There's a thin line between fortune and failure in this game. That's why I've got these boys over. You can be as good as you like, but you've got to have a story with it, something to sell. Most of these folks coming in 'ere tonight couldn't tell a good musician from a hole in the wall, but if you've got a good tale to tell they'll swear you was Orpheus on his bleedin' lute - 'scuse the French, miss."

"Like The Cat?" Ellie said, holding up a hand to let Richard know she would catch him up.

"Like The Cat," Al nodded. "He's as good as they say he is, but it's the story that sells tickets."

Ellie nodded and stepped through the double swing-doors into the half-darkness of the club.

Sarah, who had arrived with Liz ahead of the rest of them, caught her eye with an extravagant wave to guide her to their table, set up on a low balcony to the back of the room. Ellie excused her way through the busy press of tables and chairs and took her seat just as the black curtain of the stage was pulled back to reveal the band. The tall, thin man with the battered saxophone stepped forward, lifted his head, and blew; and as the first flurry of notes cascaded down to silence the noisy crowd, Ellie understood why Brix – now watching The Cat with a grin as broad as a piano keyboard – had needed just a few notes to know.

# CHAPTER 5

THE room was too loud for regular conversation, but Ellie had managed to hear enough in the few quiet moments to learn more about Georgie's friend Liz, who worked as a legal clerk in the chambers Georgie was about to join. She was good company, with a seemingly bottomless well of anecdotes about the misbehaviour of the great and good who needed the services of London's best lawyers. Ellie wasn't entirely sure Liz was meant to be broadcasting these, even if she had a storyteller's knack of bringing each scandal to vivid life.

She didn't learn much more about Sarah, as she seemed determined to keep her audience of one very much to herself. Whatever she was discussing with Richard must have been fascinating, she thought, as she laughed and smiled at his every word, moving her chair ever closer and grasping his hand as she leaned in to speak over the din of the room.

The crowd broke into a thunder of applause as a roll of Ben's drums brought one song to an end, then Clay's bass picked up the fast tempo of another. Sarah half-stood, taking a firm grip of Richard's arm.

"Oh, now this is more like it," she said, swaying her free hand in time to the music. "Richard, I absolutely insist that you dance with me to this one."

Richard's face contorted into an awkward smile. "I'm afraid I should probably cramp your style, Sarah. This sort of thing… well, it's not my forte I'm afraid. Perhaps—"

"I say! What the devil do you think you're doing?" Sarah let go of Richard's arm to turn suddenly towards where a thin, taut-faced man in an ill-fitting suit was pushing his way past the adjoining tables, clutching something to his chest.

"That villain has my evening bag!" Sarah shouted, pointing an accusatory finger in the man's direction. "Stop! Thief!"

Her call for help was lost in the sound of music and conversation, as the man tried to forcefully squeeze his way past the last of the tables to head towards the lights of the exit corridor. Richard looked between Sarah and the disappearing thief, then shook his head firmly.

"This won't do," he said decisively. "Will you excuse me, ladies?" He straightened out his trouser legs, took a deep breath then stepped up onto the table. "I do apologise," he said, stepping across the gap to the adjoining table, "I'm awfully sorry, it's something of an emergency."

Ellie watched, in bemusement, as Richard skipped quickly across the row of tables between them and the door, tiptoeing carefully among the spread of cocktail glasses and apologising profusely with each new table he disturbed. He vaulted the last with a full stretch of his long legs, to land directly in the path of the man who was now trying to hide the stolen bag under his jacket as he approached the exit.

"Sir, I am afraid I am going to have to ask you to return that bag," Richard said, holding out his hand. "I rather think that it does not belong to you."

Richard's table-hopping had drawn the attention of the crowd away from the band and towards the doorway, where the two men now stood facing each other.

"Alright, keep your 'air on," the man said, glancing past Richard towards the open door. "'Ere, if you want it so bad you can 'ave it." The man reached into his jacket then quickly pulled out his hand again, but it wasn't holding Sarah's bag. Instead, the bright ceiling lights above picked out the glint of a blade, long and thin and deadly-looking.

"Got out my way, mister, or this is for you," the man growled.

Richard instinctively stepped back, holding up his hands defensively. "Now, sir, don't be foolish. Just drop the knife and the bag, and you can get on your way."

The man brandished the knife again, beads of nervous sweat on his forehead as he edged toward Richard. "I mean it, mister. Let me past."

"I'm afraid I can't do that without the bag," Richard said, backing a little closer to the door.

"I'm telling you," the man snarled, "I'll use it. Don't think I–"

The man's words were muffled by a thick, heavy hand across his mouth as the lantern-jawed doorman stepped out of the shadow of an alcove to take the man in a tight bear-grip. The doorman twisted the man's arm to force out the knife, which fell to the floor at Richard's feet.

"I believe this belongs to you," the doorman said, restraining the thief with one powerful arm while pulling out the small, black-velvet bag from under the man's jacket and handing it to Richard.

Richard coloured slightly. "It belongs to a lady friend of mine, yes," he said.

Ellie suddenly became aware of the silence. The band had stopped playing and the audience's focus was now entirely on the events at the front door. Richard must have noticed too, as he quickly thanked the doorman and made his way – even more apologetically than before – back to the table.

A round-faced, expensively-dressed man in one of the seats put his drink down to pat him on the back as he passed and Richard nodded an awkward acknowledgement.

"Gosh, Richard," Sarah gushed, beaming widely, "that was awfully chivalrous of you. You really are quite the dashing hero."

Richard looked more awkward than ever as he sat down, forcing a smile onto his reddening face. "Well… I suppose… it's just, one ought to stand up to these things you see. It's just the proper thing to do. I had no idea the fellow was carrying a knife."

"I'm really not sure what kind of people they are letting in here," Liz said firmly. "I thought this was meant to be an exclusive event."

The band suddenly struck up again, turning heads back to the stage, as Ellie watched the bag-thief wriggling his way free of his captor's grasp to sprint out of the door before the police could arrive. As he disappeared, she saw a number of other men stand up from their places around the room and head rapidly for the exit. The chairs Richard had vaulted over were suddenly pulled in again as a heavy-set figure eased his way briskly towards their table.

"Lord Melmersby, Miss Fotheringay, please let me apologise. I am not sure how the blazes that bloke got in. I hope you are alright." Al Maguire had pushed his way through to stand over their table, clutching a particularly large bottle of champagne. "I insist you take this bottle as my way of apology, and please, if you need anything else – anything at all – you just talk to the bar staff and it's yours. I am so very sorry."

"I should think so!" Liz snapped, arms folded firmly.

"It was nothing," Richard said. "All sorted. I think we're fine now, aren't we?"

He looked at Sarah as he spoke and she responded by gripping his arm firmly, suddenly looking considerably more shaken than she had been just moments before, so much that she had to rest her head on his shoulder to recover her composure . "It was quite the fright," she said. "I feel quite shaken, but I am sure I shall feel much safer with Richard here by my side."

Ellie raised an eyebrow, but she couldn't help but feel quietly impressed by Richard's actions, even if she had the strong suspicion that Sarah was considerably more capable of looking after herself than it now suited her to show.

The band kicked into a swinging blues, and the attention of the room was now fully back on having a good time. Conversation around Ellie's table switched back to lighter topics, helped along by the full glasses of good champagne, as Georgie prompted Liz to retell the scandal of Lord Farnley and the bishop's twins.

Amusing as it was, Ellie had heard the tale earlier and so her attention wandered to the rest of the room. More people had left since the incident with the bag, and now she could see a number of empty tables all around the room. The night was drawing on, and there had been a definite change in atmosphere since the bag-snatch. She wondered if the drama hadn't sobered up a few revelers to turn in early, or at least find a quieter spot to continue their evening. With the crowd now thinner, she could see across to a small table set close to the stage, with three men sitting in it. While the other two men spoke animatedly, the third man was frantically scribbling in a small notebook and paying little attention to what was happening on the stage. It took her a second to remember why his face seemed so familiar, but as he turned his head around, she recognised him as the reporter from the Cafe Royale, Eric Prendergast. As she watched, Al Maguire approached the table, grinning acknowledgement to the first two men, but studiously ignoring Eric apart from a quick glance that looked as sharp as the knife the bag-snatcher had brandished. Al put down a bottle – smaller than the one he had given them – and walked away, his smile now replaced by a dark frown.

"Richard has very chivalrously agreed to escort me home," Sarah said loudly, pulling Ellie's attention back to the table. "I am far too shaken to return alone." She stood up, smiling sweetly at Richard as he pulled back her chair and offered his arm to escort her out, Sarah gripping it firmly in both hands as they turned out of the club door.

"I believe I shall turn in too," Liz said, pushing away a champagne flute that held its last drops. "It is frightfully late. Georgie, would you care to share a cab?"

"What about you, Ellie?" Georgie said. "I think this is the band's last number, and look, the place is nearly empty now. Are you ready to head back with us?"

Ellie looked back at the three men at the table. "Do you mind if we stay just a little longer? There's someone I'd like to talk to."

Georgie shrugged, and Liz gave out a deliberate yawn as if to show what an inconvenience it would be to get to bed so late. Ellie thanked them with a guilty grin: she wasn't entirely sure why she felt the need to talk to the reporter, but something told her she should, and she knew enough of her intuition to wonder if she wasn't about to step into the kind of trouble she seemed to have made a habit of since her arrival in England. She shivered slightly at the thought of that, then looked back to the table where the three men were sitting.

The band had finished playing, to enthusiastic applause from the now sparse crowd, and no sooner had the musicians started to put away their instruments than Eric Prendergast stood up sharply and made a bee-line straight towards Louis Luther. The Cat snarled and turned his back sharply, as Al stepped as briskly as his heavy frame would allow, up onto the side of the low stage to quickly draw the heavy black curtain and cut off the reporter's question before it could be asked.

"Excuse me," Ellie said to Liz and Georgie, "I just want to have a quick word with that man there."

She slipped quickly past the nearly empty tables and down the short flight of steps to the dancefloor, side-stepping a balding man with a thin salt-and-pepper beard and his far-too-young-for-him date as they headed for the exit.

"Hi, Eric!" she called out, and the reporter turned from trying to peer through the curtain to give her a practiced smile.

"Hi darlin'," he said, "Enjoy the show did you?"

"I did," Ellie said, ignoring his uneasy charm. "How about you?"

Eric pulled out a newspaper that he'd rolled up and stuffed in the pocket of his faded jacket. "It normally costs you tuppence to find out what I think," he said, "but I got a few copies for Al, so you can have a read if you like. My review of last night's show is on page 14."

Ellie took the paper but didn't unroll it. "I see you were trying to talk to Louis. Any luck?"

Eric shook his head wistfully. "Not yet, but he'll talk to me, I can promise you that."

Ellie felt her intuition tingle again at Eric's certainty, and she began to wonder if she shouldn't leave it at that. Maybe she'd spent too many afternoons in Mrs Garnet's tea-shoppe and had developed a taste for that baker's brand of gossip, she thought, or maybe she just had the sense that if trouble was always so determined to find her she might be better meeting it head-on, and on her own terms.

"He's an interesting character, I guess," Ellie said. "What are you trying to talk to him about?"

Eric ignored the question. "Interesting is the word," he said. "All sorts of tales about that one."

Ellie could see Al watching them from the doorway of a dark corridor that led down into the heart of the building. From his impatient expression, she got the impression he was waiting for Eric to leave.

"What kind of tales?" Ellie turned to look back at the table where Liz and Georgie still sat, finishing the last of the champagne. She held up a hand to tell them she wouldn't be too long, as Liz made a point of looking down at her watch.

"Man of mystery," Eric said. "Some people say he got his gift from a voodoo witch doctor in New Orleans, others reckon he stole Jessica—"

"Jessica?"

"His saxophone," Eric said, in a way that suggested she should have known that. "Some people say it's a magic charm that gives him his gift."

Ellie let out a sharp laugh. "I've learned not to believe those kinds of stories, the real world's trouble enough without the need for magic."

Eric laughed too. "Ah yes, Ellie Blaine. I read about you and that business with the professor in Yorkshire; made for great copy. And you're right. There's a few good stories about the Cat but of course it's all hocus-pocus made to drum up business. And anyway, fact is often more interesting than fiction, I find."

Ellie looked at him quizzically. "Do you know something about Louis?"

"I'm not really–" Eric stopped at the weight of a heavy hand on his shoulder and turned with a greasy grin. "Al – just the man I wanted to see!"

Al did not look like he wanted to see Eric, but he put on a half-convincing display of good humour. "It might be time to leave now, Eric. We're closing up."

Ellie glanced at the table where Eric's two companions looked up quickly from their conversation. One of the men now stood to walk towards them, his broad, heavily-mustached face set in an even broader smile.

Al beamed back. "Spats, you old devil, hope you enjoyed the show."

"Big Al! Those boys were as good as they say, you've outdone yourself."

The two men shook hands, each seeming to fight to get the firmer grip, with 'Spats' going for a double-hander to press his in harder.

"I've done well enough," Al said. "So if you've come to gloat, maybe check my door receipts first."

"Gloat?" Ellie said, looking between them.

"Seems like we won the 'Battle of the Blues'," Spats grinned. "At least according to Eric here, and Eric is the voice of jazz in London, so I'll take that as official."

"Page 14," Eric said, answering Ellie's questioning look with a nod at the paper.

She unfurled the copy of The Post, quickly flicking through it to the right page. There, just below an advert claiming to have found a cure for 'housemaid's knee', she saw the headline: *'Louis is the Cat's Whiskers, but Tommy's Band is Tops.'*

"So—" Ellie started, but someone else finished her question for her, a lot more forcefully than she intended.

"Where is he? Where is that cloth-eared, no-good hack who wrote this garbage? Is that him? What the hell does he know about jazz?"

Brix had burst through the door from the back rooms and was angrily jabbing a rolled-up copy of the newspaper in the direction of Eric, who raised a nervous hand to indicate he'd found the right man.

Brix furiously tore open the paper, to spit out the words as he read them. "What is this? *'But it was Tommy's band that had that hot swinging sound that really made the crowd want to get up and dance'.* You wouldn't know swing if it swung up behind you and hit you on your—"

"Hey Brix, man. Good to see you!"

The third man from Eric's table had now joined them, a tall, blond man with a gentle, open face and a broad Chicago accent.

Brix sighed deeply, composing himself. "Hey Tommy, good to see you. Can you believe this trash?"

Tommy smiled diplomatically. "Ah, it's just someone's opinion. You guys were swinging hot tonight."

Brix gave a nod of appreciation for the comment. "Maybe you should tell this ink-head that," he said. "He don't know jazz from jello. Since when does a Limey know anything about swing?"

Liz and Georgie, either bored of waiting or more likely intrigued by the raised voices that would have carried across the room, now walked down to join the growing huddle.

"I thought you were all rather splendid," Georgie said, addressing Brix who simply frowned in response. "I'm sure there's room in this big city of ours for two great bands."

"I want him out of here, and I don't want to see him again," Brix snarled, jabbing a finger at Eric. "If I do, I won't be responsible for what happens to him!" The bandleader turned sharply and stormed back towards the door, deliberately tossing the paper in a small wastepaper bin as he went.

Eric smiled sheepishly. "Don't worry, I'll be out of here in a second. I just wanted to see if I could have a word with Al before I go."

Al shook his head. "If you want me to talk The Cat into speaking to you, you're out of luck. He won't talk to anyone, and certainly not you."

"Maybe," Eric said, "but if you've got a minute perhaps we could talk about it anyway. I have a feeling you'd be very interested to hear what I've got to say."

Al growled quietly. "I'll see you in my office in a minute, you can wait for me there. We need to get the place cleaned up."

Eric gave an exaggerated bow and headed through the door that Brix had just slammed behind himself.

"He's a cheeky so-and-so," Al said, puffing out his cheeks. "But sadly he's quite influential. I'll give him five minutes then I'll kick him out, if Brix doesn't find him first."

"Where's the rest of the band?" Liz asked, looking eagerly around.

Al shrugged. "Ben and Clay were in the dressing room last time I saw them, no idea where Louis has taken himself off to. He keeps himself to himself."

Liz looked disappointed and began to pull out her watch again. Tommy leaned in, gesturing with his thumb towards the door. "I'll see if I can persuade them to step out for a minute," he said. "I can find my way, if that's alright with you Al?"

"Be my guest," Al said casually. "Right. Spats, I'll catch you later – the rest of you better get on your way, I need this place closed and I need to get to my bed. I'm giving Eric five minutes, no more. Once Tommy gets back, you need to make yourselves scarce."

Al followed Tommy through the door at the back of the room, side-stepping quickly as a short, worried-looking middle-aged woman clutching a mop and bucket came out from the dark corridor, putting down her load to start wiping down one of the tables.

"I'm not sure we should be staying after all," Liz said, nodding towards the cleaner. "Come along, or we shall never find a cab."

"I'll catch you up," Ellie said. "Give me ten minutes, and I'll be out."

Liz shook her head and took Georgie's arm to pull her, semi-reluctantly, along towards the exit where the doorman ushered them forwards and out. "Ten minutes, Ellie, or we shall leave without you!" she called back.

Ellie shrugged at Spats as the two of them stood, silent for a moment, the room empty but for the clatter of glasses as the cleaning lady picked up.

"You a friend of Al's?" Spats said, breaking the silence.

Ellie shook her head, suddenly conscious that she really had no reason to still be there but for her curiosity around what Eric might know about Louis. "I know Eric," she said, colouring slightly at the white lie. She decided to change the subject before he asked any more about her acquaintance with the reporter. "You must be pleased with your review?"

Spats shrugged. "Yeah, but I'd be happier with Al's crowd," he said. "We didn't even do half the numbers. He's obviously found where the jazz crowd are hiding, 'cos they sure aren't coming to see Tommy."

"Maybe after Eric's article…" Ellie said.

"Maybe," Spats said. "I wasn't sure jazz was big enough here yet, but Al put his money where his mouth is and bought these guys in. I couldn't afford them. Nor could he, I'm sure. But he took the risk and I can't begrudge him his success. Reviews are nice, but ticket sales are all that matters to the likes of me and Al, and he's won that, fair play to him."

Spats turned away from the conversation to nod towards the door, where Tommy Marvin now appeared holding out his upturned hands. "No sign of The Cat," he said. "Or the other guys. Dressing room is empty." He looked around the quiet room. "Where'd everybody go?"

Ellie sighed, suddenly aware she might be outstaying her welcome. "I should probably... it's time I went."

The sound of breaking glass turned everyone's head suddenly towards one of the tables set against the back wall of the club. The cleaning lady was down on her knees, gathering up the shattered remains of a champagne glass, muttering to herself.

"Can I help you with that?" Ellie said, stepping slightly towards her.

"Oh no, miss," the woman said with a swift wave of her hand. "Don't you bother yourself, just clumsy old me. I'll get a rag to gather this up."

The woman stood stiffly, clutching a knee as she did, and hurried towards the back rooms door in a series of quick, shuffling steps.

"Thank you for your time," Ellie said to the two men. "I'd better go and catch Liz and Georgie up before they leave without me. I'm not sure I know where—"

Ellie's words were cut short by a piercing scream. She turned with Al and Tommy towards the darkened door, just as the cleaning lady reemerged, trembling violently from head to foot and wringing her hands in her beer-stained apron.

"Are you alright, love?" Spats said.

The woman shook her head, eyes wide with bewilderment. "Oh sir, no sir," she said. "I really… I don't know… oh my, I ain't seen nothin' like it."

"What is it? Is everything alright?" Ellie stepped towards the shaking woman, putting a gentle hand on her arm.

"It's in the broom cupboard, miss. I just went to get a rag, that's all."

"What is?"

"A body, miss. There's a dead man in the broom cupboard."

# CHAPTER 6

"ONE of you in this room is a murderer." The inspector pointed a sharp finger at each person in turn as he scanned the awkward huddle set around the low stage. "My job – and just so you know, I always get the job done – is to find out which one of you it is. Until I do, you are all suspects, so pick your words very carefully."

Ellie glanced at the sobbing, frail figure of the cleaning woman, desperately clinging to her mop as she hunched in her chair, shaking like a particularly flimsy leaf. She imagined she might have ruled her out as a suspect; she didn't look like she had the strength to wring out a wet floor cloth, never mind to strangle a fully-grown man. And Eric Prendergast is – was – about twice her size.

"What about The Cat?" Georgie said, holding up her hand and speaking as though she were back behind her desk at Cheltenham Ladies College and addressing her least-favourite teacher.

"You're saying you think it might have been a cat now?" The inspector gurned. "What in the name of–"

"Not a cat," Georgie sighed, rolling her eyes. "The Cat – Louis… thingy."

"Louis Luther," Al put in. "They call him The Cat. Sax player. He was here too. Well, he should have been."

"Cat likes to keep his own company," Brix growled. "No idea where he takes himself to after a show. Don't care none either, long as he comes back for the next show."

"I will want to speak to this… Cat," the inspector said. "So you'd better let me know the minute he turns up, or there might not be a next show."

The inspector had introduced himself as DI Rex Kinkaid in a manner that suggested to Ellie she should know who he was. He was a short, shabbily-dressed man in his mid-50s. His hard, sallow face, red-rimmed eyes and sandpaper-rough voice seemed to have been shaped by the constant chain of cigarettes he worked his way through as he grilled them. And perhaps, Ellie thought, his attitude was shaped by too many years of dealing with the worst of people, as he spoke to everyone as if their guilt was already assured.

"Now, let's get this straight," DI Kinkaid said, wetting a stubby thumb with his tongue to flip back over his notebook. "The deceased had gone to Mr Maguire's office to wait for him; Mr Maguire—"

Al pointed to himself. "Me?"

DI Kinkaid raised his eyes slowly to look over the top of his notebook. "Unless anyone else here has the same name, yes, you. You say the deceased wanted to talk to you. In private. I wonder what it was he wanted to talk to you about?"

Al shrugged. "He said he wanted to talk to me about Louis. He seemed to have some notion he had a story he wanted to write about him. I told him to wait in my office, but when I got there he wasn't there."

"A story you say?" the inspector said, looking up fully now and lowering his notebook. "I will definitely need to speak to this Cat of yours." He turned sharply to face Tommy Marvin who was looking back over his shoulder in the direction of the two white-coated men busily removing the unfortunate reporter on a squeaky trolley they were having some trouble maneuvering up the dancefloor steps. "You, Mr Marvin," the inspector continued, shaking his head as the men nearly tipped the trolley over on their way up. "You were also in the back rooms when the murder occurred."

Tommy nodded. "I was, and so were Clay and Ben and Brix, but ain't none of us a killer; I'm as sure of that as I am that you're wasting your time keeping us here."

DI Lochner gave a cynical smile. "You'd be surprised how many times I've heard a man tell me I'm wasting my time – usually about ten minutes before I get him put in cuffs and taken away." He turned to face Ellie and Georgie. "And you ladies, and you Mr Corliss, you say you were out here when the murder happened? None of you slipped into the backroom for a minute did you? It doesn't take too long to strangle a man, no, not long at all."

"Well you obviously know a lot more about strangling than any of us do, Mr Kinkaid," Georgie said sharply. "It's not a subject I'm familiar with, I'm afraid – never had the call for it. But if you are trying to get to the bottom of this case rather than simply throwing accusations at all and sundry you might do well to ask young Ellie to assist. She's rather the dab hand at solving murders. You may have heard of Professor Berens and that ghastly business last year with the druids and whatnot."

"Ah yes," DI Lochner said, grinning in a way that made Georgie narrow her eyes. "Ellie Blaine – I knew I'd heard that name before. I read about that. Seems you have a habit of being in places where people meet a sticky end."

Georgie coughed. "And a habit of solving the crime when the police failed miserably. She's a consulting detective, you know, for our local force."

"Consultant to a detective," Ellie corrected her with a sly smile.

DI Kinkaid put his hands together. "Very impressive," he said. "Consultant to a detective, hey? Well, here's the thing, Miss Blaine, consultant to a detective." He stepped forward and put his face close enough to hers that she instinctively pulled her head back at the strong scent of cheap cologne and stale cigarettes. "I have been a detective in the great city of London for nearly 20 years, and in that time I 've solved nearly twice that number of murders. So excuse me if I am not quite at the point where I need the assistance of someone who managed to stumble her way through Yorkshire bogs just long enough to be rescued by the village bobbies; who, let's be honest, had probably never dealt with anything more serious than urchins scrumping apples before. This is the big city, love, not the Dales. It's no place for amateur sleuths, and – if I might be so bold – no place for ladies to go poking around neither. This is men's work."

Ellie caught sight of Georgie's face as it threatened to turn from red to purple, and quickly stepped in before her friend could go fully volcanic and drop them all in it. "Well," she said as softly as she could, "I'm sure you know what you are doing, so we won't talk about it again. Have you finished questioning us yet, because it's very late and I'm sure you wouldn't want delicate ladies like us travelling home too late in this big, bad city of yours."

"I'll drive you back," Al said. "It's the least I can do, after what you've seen here tonight."

DI Kinkaid frowned. "Very well, you can all leave. But I will insist that you remain where you can be contacted until inquiries are complete. I will need to talk to all of you again, you can be sure of that."

The inspector saw himself out, brushing aside Al's attempts to show him politely to the door. He allowed himself one more suspicious glance at the assembled suspects, then firmly shut the door behind himself.

Al let out a deep sigh. "Well, this doesn't bode too well for the rest of the tour," he said, rubbing his face to put some colour back in it.

Clay shrugged. "He said we gotta stay in contact, you got telephones in this country right?"

Al shook his head. "I don't know – it's a serious matter." He sat down heavily in the chair beside the cleaning lady, who gave a sharp squeak and dropped her mop in shock at the sudden movement. "If the tour is called off it'll be a disaster. I've booked everywhere ahead; no refunds. It was bad enough with Paris – at least they were good about the money."

Ellie looked quizzically at Al, slumped in the chair with his hands now on the side of his head. "You're going to Paris?"

Al nodded without looking up. "We were. I had the whole thing lined up: London first, then a grand tour of England and finishing off with four nights in Paris. It's the hottest jazz scene outside of the US, you know. Would have made a killing there." He held his empty hands out in exasperation.

"So why aren't you—"

"It's Cat," Brix mumbled, chewing on a half-eaten toothpick. "Cat won't go to Paris, and Brix won't go without Cat. No Cat, no show."

"Why ever not?" Georgie said incredulously. "Paris is simply divine."

Clay shrugged. "He didn't say. Reckons it's a bad place, that's all. We all tried to talk him round – trust me, I would love to go to Paris. But when The Cat makes up his mind, he makes up his mind."

"Well," Georgie said firmly. "I am of a mind to get to my bed, and I'm afraid I am just as stubborn, so shall we be going?"

"I'll get my car ready," Al said, finally standing up again. "It's been a hell of a night, and I'll be glad to see the end of it."

Ellie bid a polite goodbye to Tommy, Brix, Clay and Ben and followed with Liz and Georgie through the side door of the club to where Al's black sedan car waited, with the club owner holding the door for them to step in.

"24 Lavenham Mews," Liz said, the moment she sat down in the back seat. "Mayfair. Do you know it?"

Al nodded. "I do – we'll have you home in a jiffy."

The car turned slowly around the corner of Greek Street and round into Shaftesbury Avenue. Liz was doing her best to keep her eyes from closing, jolted open by the occasional bump in the rough road surface. Ellie watched the darkened buildings roll by, the usually bustling streets of London's theatreland now empty but for the occasional shadow of a beggar huddled in a doorway or the scuttle of a street dog looking for scraps.

"I say! Is that the Cat fellow?" Georgie had been looking out of the other window at the opposite side of the street and now all heads in the car turned to follow her pointing finger. "There, look, walking down that way."

Ellie caught sight of a tall, immaculately dressed man as he turned into the darkness of one the side streets that threaded through the heart of Soho.

Al grunted. "It's him alright. Wonder where's been? On second thoughts, I'd rather not know."

"I wonder what poor Eric Prendergast wanted to talk to him about?" Ellie said. She'd meant to say it to herself but, half-asleep now, the words came out anyway.

"He's an odd character," Al said. "Not sure I entirely trust him, but he's been no trouble for me, so I'm not going to speculate."

"Eric told me there were tales he'd stolen… Jessica?" Ellie said, reaching for the memory of the name the reporter had given her. "Do you think there's anything in that?"

"Who on earth is—" Georgie started.

"His saxophone," Al cut in. "She's practically a part of him, he won't play without her. Seems to think there's some magic in her, or some such," he said, suddenly honking the car's horn at a stray dog that had wandered into the road to sniff at something unpleasant looking on the tarmac. "I think he likes to create a bit of an air of mystery about himself. It's all showbusiness – voodoo and black magic and so on, you know the kind of thing."

"Unfortunately we do," Georgie said, "And, nonsense or not, it tends to end with people being bumped off and us getting dragged into it. What kind of tall tale are we dealing with now?"

"Oh you know the sort of thing," Al said, turning sharply into a narrow road and gesturing to Liz that he was close to her home. "Apparently the saxophone belonged to some young musician who sold his soul for it. Louis is meant to have stolen it, or done the fella in, or some such. 'Course, no one can ever say who this was, or where it happened, or when. But then facts like that do tend to get in the way of a good showbusiness story. Either way, he's got the sax now and it's why he plays so well, if you believe that sort of thing. Here you go, love."

Al had pulled up outside a smart two-storey mews house and stepped out to open the door for Liz, then got back in to turn fully in his seat and address Georgie and Ellie.

"Cat don't seem like a killer to me," he said.

"But what if Mr Prendergast had found something out about him? He seems to be the only one who might have a motive," Ellie said.

"I would say Brix had a motive too," Georgie said. "He practically took poor Ben's head off with a watch over a bit of drumming; who knows what he might do to someone who gave him a bad review?"

"I'm not sure a bad review is motive for murder," Ellie said, frowning.

"You don't know Brix!" Al said, turning back to the road as he navigated a wide bend. "No, but seriously, he's not that bad. At least I don't think he is?"

"We'll get out here, thank you," Georgie said suddenly as the car pulled into the wide, grand space of Grosvenor Square. "My little place is just here."

"Thank you for the lift," Ellie said. "And be careful. DI Kinkaid was right about one thing – whoever the killer was, he was in the club tonight. And if I've learned one thing over the last year or so it's that they never seem to stop at just one."

# CHAPTER 7

"I WONDER," Richard said with a sly smile, "if there's a chance you might go somewhere one day and there not be a murder immediately in your wake." His face quickly dropped to a more sombre expression at Ellie's unspoken response. "But seriously, what a terrible business. Do you have any idea what might have happened?"

Ellie shrugged. "None. Except that someone at the club wanted that reporter out of the way. I'm not sure the police here are that keen on me thinking any more about it. And to be honest, I'm not sure I am either. I was kind of hoping this might be a nice break."

"And so it shall be, I promise," Richard said firmly, putting out his hand to give Ellie her coat.

"The cab is outside and London is yours to explore."

Georgie had left Ellie to herself while she spent the day at her new chambers, and instructed Richard to see to it that Ellie was kept entertained. Lord Melmersby seemed happy enough to take on that task, and had planned out an itinerary he was sure would show her the best side of England's capital.

"We'll start off at the British Museum,' he said. "Absolutely fascinating place. I could spend all day in The Egyptian Sculpture Gallery alone, and you will finally be able to see the treasure that that scoundrel Ralph Berens nearly killed you for. Then we'll pop on the Tube to the Tower – full of history; I shall be your guide. Then I thought perhaps, after lunch, we might pop into Oxford Street, do a little shopping. Not my area of expertise, I'm afraid, but we can't fail to find something delightful there I'm sure."

Ellie smiled. "That all sounds swell," she said, turning to allow Richard to help her on with her coat. "That should keep me out of trouble, for the day at least."

\* \* \*

"No, so Anne of Cleeves, she was the fourth one. The poor girl had the most unfortunate countenance, it seems, so Henry saw her off with a nice pension. Divorced, beheaded, died, divorced, beheaded, survived – that's the way to remember them."

Ellie nodded politely. Richard had taken his duties as tour guide to heart and was spending the journey from the Tower of London to Oxford Street giving her a potted guide to what seemed to be the entirety of British history. It was certainly thorough, she thought, but after the museum and the Tower her head was already so full of historical facts that she was running out of places to put new ones, and she was relieved when Richard nodded towards the door of the carriage.

"Out here," he said firmly. "It's a little walk to Bank Station to get our connection. I shall tell you of Henry's storied progeny once we are on the Central Line."

Ellie forced a grin. "I'm sure his... progeny is fascinating," she said, trying to read Richard's face and unsure she meant to draw the reaction she could see. "But maybe it could wait until lunch?"

Richard frowned, then nodded. "Of course. I'm probably boring you terribly, I do apologise."

"No," Ellie insisted, suddenly conscious of the slight flush in Richard's cheeks. "It's just a bit noisy on the train, and there's a lot to take in. I'd rather hear you properly."

Richard's expression gave the impression he was unconvinced by her explanation, but he gestured for her to take the stairs ahead of him, putting himself between her and the jostle of the busy late-morning crowd. As they stepped up the short flight, a young woman coming down the opposite way threw a curious glance at Richard, then did a double-take that broke into a broad, grateful grin.

"Dr Richard!" she called cheerfully. "Well bless my soul. What a treat it is to see you!" The woman stepped across to the thin metal rail that separated the two flights and reached over to pull Richard into an embrace that drew an awkward grimace that might have been meant as a smile.

"You remember me, don't you, sir?" the woman said, standing back to show herself more clearly.

"Of course," Richard said, shaking the memory back into his head. "Jenny isn't it? And how is little…?"

"Dickie?" the woman said with a smile. "Named him after you, sir, so I did. If that's alright with you?"

"Well…yes. I suppose it would make little difference now if it wasn't, but I am flattered all the same. How is the young fellow?"

"Healthy as a butcher's dog, and just as loud and messy," the woman said. "But I wouldn't have him any other way."

"Delighted to hear it, Jenny," Richard said, tipping his hat. "And glad to see you looking so well."

"Got a job now, I have," the woman said, suddenly standing a little taller. "Nufin' special, just working a bakery down Lambeth way, but they don't mind about my… situation and whatnot. Even let me bring little Dickie in on the days when its quieter."

"Wonderful," Richard said. "As it should be. Well, good day to you Jenny, we must be on our way. Do give my regards to young Dickie."

"Oh I will," the woman said, then turned to Ellie. "You got yourself a real diamond there, miss. Proper gent. One day I shall tell my Dickie what a gentleman he was named for, and I hope he grows up half the man."

The woman gave a subtle curtsy, then a gentle finger wave to Richard as she headed on her way down the stairs to the platform. Ellie raised an eyebrow, looking first to the woman and then to Richard.

"A patient of mine," he said in answer to the question her face was asking. "Mother and baby doing well, that's what I like to see."

Ellie looked at Richard for a moment. "She didn't seem the type to be—"

"Type?" Richard said, scowling slightly.

"I mean…" She hesitated. "I thought… well Georgie says…"

"That I'm too expensive for the likes of her?"

Ellie bit her lip. "Well… yes."

Richard took a shallow breath. "I suppose I am. Most of the time. But I like to give a little back, where I can. One must do what one can, with the tools one is given."

"You helped her out then?"

Richard shrugged. "My father's estate left me rather a lot of money, a lot more than I need, frankly. He also left me with a debt to pay that is far greater. After Lucy… well, after what I learned of what he did to her mother, I thought perhaps his money might be better spent putting right the wrongs he did in life. There are many women in the position my father put Lucy's mother in, and it seems right that he should pay to support them in a way he never had the decency to do when he was with us."

"What a wonderful thing to do," Ellie said, putting her hand to Richard's arm. "You are full of surprises."

Richard's cheeks coloured faintly. "Well, as I say, one should do what one can. I'm sure anyone else would do the same in my circumstances."

Ellie shook her head. "I'm not so sure of that," she said. "Anyway, we really should get some lunch. I want to hear more about Henry and his progeny."

Richard let out a short, sharp laugh. "Very well," he said. "Though there is a lot to tell, so you should be careful what you ask for."

\* \* \*

"So, how was our dear Richard?" Georgie asked, as she struggled off a shoe made a little too tight from the long walk from her chambers back to her townhouse. "I suppose he gave you the full run-down on London from caveman days to the automobile? I should have warned you, history is one of his favourite subjects."

"Mmm," Ellie said, swallowing a mouthful of soda water as she handed a glass to Georgie. "He was his usual self, only more… surprising."

"Surprising?" Georgie said, lifting her glass in salute to Ellie. "Richard is many wonderful things, but rarely surprising. What's the old boy been up to?"

"Did you know about his work with… what do they call them? Fallen women?"

Georgie laughed. "Ha! Well, yes, they do call them that. But then when most men put women on an impossibly narrow pedestal is it any surprise that a few of them fall off? Yes, I know all about that. He's a good sort, is old Richard, but we knew that already."

"He never talks about it," Ellie said.

"Well, dear thing," Georgie said, dropping down into a well-padded leather armchair and putting her stockinged feet on a small footstool, "he rarely talks about much. Apart from history, if you get him started. The truth is, Richard is that rare breed of man who does good work for the work's sake, not to gain points in some high-society virtue contest. Besides, his usual clientele are rather proud of the exclusivity of working with London's most in-demand doctor, and I rather think their noses might be put out of joint if they discovered that his patients included the 'wrong sort' of lower class lady as well as marquises and bishops."

"Well, I'm kind of proud of him," Ellie said. "It's a good thing to do."

"Oh, absolutely. Perhaps if you get him in the right mood he might take you to the clinic he set up in the East End. It's a small place, just a few staff. But all paid for and managed by our dear Richard. Here – pour me another one and we shall drink to our philanthropic friend."

Ellie grinned and stepped over to the glass cabinet where Georgie kept her impressive collection of spirits, reaching in for the half-empty bottle of Plymouth Gin. As she popped the stopper, her head turned to the sound of Georgie's door bell ringing brightly.

"Now who on earth could that be at this time?" Georgie said. "I'm not expecting anyone, and look at the state of me."

Georgie quickly threw on a house robe that hung over the back of one of the other chairs and marched purposefully to the door that led out into the open, shared foyer of the imposing building in which Georgie had made her London bolt-hole. As she cautiously opened the door she was surprised to see a face that was now familiar, but quite unexpected nonetheless.

"Mr Clayton? Clay? What on earth brings you here?"

Clay dropped his head. "I do apologise for callin' on you so unexpected Miss Georgie. I got your address from Mr Maguire, I hope I ain't puttin' you to no great inconvenience?"

"Not at all," Georgie said, stepping back to open the door wider. "Come in, come in. Can I get you a drink?"

Clay shook his head. "Not at this time, Miss Georgie…"

"Please, call me Georgie. None of this "Miss" nonsense. I'm not a preparatory school teacher," Georgie said.

Clay laughed. "Sure thing, Georgie." He caught sight of Ellie, who looked just as puzzled as Georgie had felt by Clay's arrival. He lifted his head to acknowledge her. "Truth is, I was hoping to catch you, Ellie."

"Me?" Ellie said, pointing curiously at herself and looking at Georgie for clarity she couldn't give her.

"Yeah, you see, I heard about you being some kind of private dick, and I ain't got too much time for the police, so I thought I'd come see if you could help."

"With the murder of Mr Prendergast?" Ellie said, putting down her glass on the cabinet top.

"Not with that, no," Clay said, taking a deep breath. "Something else has happened, something bad."

"I say, has there been another murder?" Georgie gasped.

Clay shook his head sombrely. "Worse than that."

"What could possibly be worse than someone being killed?" Georgie said.

Clay looked at Ellie, then back at Georgie. "Oh, someone's been killed – only it ain't a person this time."

"What do you mean?" Ellie said. "Who's been killed?"

"Jessica," Clay said, shaking his head more firmly. "Someone has gone and killed old Jessica."

# CHAPTER 8

ELLIE hadn't been so sure the destruction of a saxophone was quite as bad as a murder, but, judging from Cat's reaction, now she wasn't so sure. He certainly seemed to have taken it as badly as a bereavement and was slumped in his chair in the small, dark dressing room of the Blue Parakeet – the rise and fall of his back reflected in the array of illuminated mirrors that lined the back wall.

"I just can't accept it, no I can't accept it all. She's gone. Who would do that to her?" Cat looked up, glancing between Ellie, Clay, Brix and Ben as if one of them might have the answer.

"What did they do to it...her," Ellie said, correcting herself quickly at sight of Clay's grimace.

"Looks like someone took a hammer to her," Clay said. "A big one. Ain't no fixin' her, not now."

"She's gone," Cat said again. "I don't know what… it's like I lost a limb or somethin'. I ain't myself no more, not now. Jessica!" He half-sobbed the name, burying his head in his hands.

Ben put a consoling arm to Cat's shoulder, while Brix's expression stayed as granite-hard as ever, though Ellie could see he was chewing his toothpick just a little faster than normal.

"It's got to be Tommy, right?" Ben said, almost apologetically.

"Tommy?" Ellie said.

"Right," Ben said, looking at Brix for approval and getting no movement from the granite. "Cat took his place in the band; he's bound to be sore. Tommy's in town. It's got to be him. Hey – maybe he did that reporter guy in as well. I bet–"

Brix took his toothpick out of his mouth. "Tommy is a class act," he growled. "You should show some respect."

"I just meant–" Ben started.

"What you mean to do and what you get right ain't often the same thing," Brix snarled. "If I hear you badmouth Tommy again you and that sax of Cat's are going to have a lot in common."

"Don't you… don't you threaten me," Ben stammered. "I'm sick of you trying to push me round. I'll–"

Brix stepped forward, uncomfortably close to Ben's face and the younger man took a half step back. "You'll what, Ben?" Brix said, taking the toothpick out to point at Ben's face.

Ben lifted his head to try to look a little taller, but Ellie could see his hands were shaking. "I'll… I'll tell my pa."

Brix let out a bitter laugh. "Oh, listen to that. Daddy's boy is going to go cryin' to Papa. And what do you think Daddy will do, Benny boy?"

"What are you going to do," Ben said, trying, not particularly successfully, Ellie thought, to sound confident, "when his money stops coming in, and you have to go looking for a new deal?"

Brix's lip curled. "Let me tell you something, Benny boy. Sure, I get a good deal from your pappy, but he gets a good deal from me too. There's a hundred other music men with deep pockets out there that would snap me in a heartbeat. But you? If you so much as breathe a single bad word about me to your papa, you will be out of this band faster than you can mess up a paradiddle. And you won't just be out the band, you'll be out of the business. You forget who you are talking to – there's not a band from Tulsa to Timbuktu that would even let you listen to one of their records if I told them not to. You better learn your place, boy. I been trying to teach you where that is, but you ain't never been a good learner."

Ellie decided it might be a good time to take the conversation back to the reason she was here. "Where was the sax when it was… attacked? That might give us a clue as to what happened."

"She was just here," Cat said mournfully. "In the dressing room. We was all set to get to our afternoon rehearsal, but when I come in to get her she was... she was gone. I can't even look at her now, not like that. I can't play no more. Not without Jessica." He buried his head in his hands again.

Brix glared at Cat. "Well, Cat, you're gonna have to or else we've got no show."

"Sorry if this is... insensitive," Ellie said, keeping a hush in her voice as she pulled Clay into the far corner of the room, away from Cat. "Couldn't he just get another sax? I mean, for the show?"

Clay glanced cautiously over Ellie's shoulder. "He's very particular about what he plays. Won't play just any old sax, it's got to have a soul, he says. We'll need to find him a good one – more than a good one, a special one – and that won't be easy. No, that won't be easy at all."

"So, who do we know was in the club at the time? Who might have had the opportunity to do this?" Ellie said.

"Well," Clay said. "There was me, Brix, Ben–"

His voice was cut short by a loud rat-a-tat on the dressing room door.

"Come in," Brix grunted. "But this better be important."

The door opened slowly, and a head popped around its edge wearing a sympathetic smile. "Hey, how you all doing? I just called on Al earlier and I heard the news, I've come to see Cat."

Brix's hard face suddenly softened as much as it could, which wasn't much. "Tommy! My man! Good to see you. Cat's hit pretty bad." Brix nodded to the still-slumped figure in the corner chair.

Tommy stepped fully in and Ellie could see he was carrying a curved, black case in his left hand. "Louis, man, I am so sorry buddy. Ain't that a kick in the face?"

Cat looked up, the faintest trace of a smile on his face. "Tommy. Man, I ain't ever felt so blue. I just don't get it. Why? Jessica." He sighed the name out and put down his head again.

Tommy set the case down and stepped over to Cat, taking his shoulders in both hands to try to lift his head up. "Hey, Louis, I feel it man," he said. "You and Jessica, you were a great team."

"She's gone," Cat said, mournfully looking up to fix Tommy's eyes.

"She's gone," Tommy confirmed. "But you're still here, Cat. And you're still gonna play better than anyone I know, you just gotta do it with another lady."

Cat sniffed. "I don't know where I'm gonna find another girl like her."

Tommy smiled, then reached down for the case he had brought in, lifting her carefully up to place down on the shelf that lined the room below the wall mirrors and clicking open its three brass fasteners.

"Well," he said, lifting the lid. "She ain't quite as classy a girl as ol' Jessica, but she's a lady and she sings real sweet. I guess she might help you take your mind off of Jessica, a little at least."

As the case opened, Ellie could see the scattered reflections of mirror lights shining brightly in the polished brass of a gleaming saxophone. She saw Ben blush deeply and Clay staring at the case with his mouth wide open.

"Tommy! Man, you can't... no, I can't take her," Cat started.

"You can, Louis, and you will. I ain't takin' no for an answer," Tommy said.

Even Brix looked shocked. "Is that Sweet Lisa?" he said, staring just as hard as Clay.

Tommy nodded. "Yeah, ain't she a knock-out?"

Cat stood up, facing Tommy directly. "Man, you can't give me Sweet Lisa, she's your baby."

Tommy grinned. "Call it a loan – just until you find another one that can stand up to Jessica," he said. "She's the finest sax I ever played, and it's gonna be a real treat for her to sing for the finest sax player I ever met. I'll just use my—"

Tommy's words were squeezed out as Cat threw his arms around him and pulled him into a heavy embrace. Ben blushed even harder, trying his best not to catch Brix's eyes as the bandleader threw him a hard look.

"Man, you are the best. The real best. If there's anything I can ever do—" Cat started.

"Just play her, Louis. Just play her like I know you can, like only you can. And look after her, you hear me? You treat her real nice."

Cat nodded, then pulled Tommy back in for another hug.

The slamming of a door down the corridor and the sound of raised voices broke the silent awe of the room. Even through the closed dressing room door, Ellie could recognise the tension in the voice of Al Maguire.

"You're being unreasonable," he was saying, almost shouting. "I've told you, just give me a few more weeks, I'll be in a position to settle everything. I'll make twice what you're asking. I just need a bit of understanding from your end."

She couldn't make out the quieter voices that responded, but Al sighed loud enough as whoever he was talking to turned away to the sound of tapping footsteps of hard-soled shoes on a wooden floor and a heavy door being closed firmly.

"What's up with Al?" Ellie said.

Clay shrugged. "Saw him just now, talking with two gents in his office. Real smart; starched collars and business suits kinda gents. He didn't look happy. He don't sound happy."

The dressing room door suddenly swung open without a knock, and Ellie could see Al was sweating heavily and looking even more pink in the face than normal as he shuffled in awkwardly to fill the last part of the small room.

"Everything ok here?" Brix said, pulling out his toothpick again.

"Everything is fine," Al said, in a tone that suggested it wasn't. "Or it would be if we didn't have a massive problem with our biggest star. What are we going to do, Brix? If Cat can't play, the show is over. The tour is over."

Clay nodded to Tommy. "Problem fixed, chief. Ol' Tommy here saved the day, rode into the rescue like the Sixth Cavalry."

Al stared at Brix incredulously.

"Tommy's given Cat his sax," Brix said with the barest nod of his head. "The show goes on."

Al looked baffled for a moment, shaking his head as if he couldn't believe what he was hearing. "Tommy?" he said, looking for clarification.

Tommy grinned. "I'm letting him look after Sweet Lisa for a little while," he said. "Just happy to help."

Al paused to catch a breath that seemed to have escaped him for a second. "But what about Jessica?" he said, staring at Cat nervously. "Cat can't play without Jessica."

"I'm gonna make it through," Cat said, firmly patting Tommy's back, "thanks to my buddy here. I just don't know what to say, Tommy, you're the best, buddy, just the best."

"Well," Al said, wiping his brow with a white kerchief he pulled from his jacket pocket, "ain't that something." He pushed the sweat-soaked cloth back into his pocket and puffed out his cheeks. "Look – I'm not going to beat about the bush. Those chaps I was talking to... I need this tour to be a success. I need nothing else to go wrong, because right now I'm at my wits end, I..."

Ellie put out her hand to offer Al a glass of water that he looked like he needed right then. He took it without thanks and swallowed the contents in one gulp.

"I've got a lot riding on this tour," he said. "Just… put on a good show. I can't afford for anything else to go wrong."

Brix slapped Al firmly on his arm as he moved towards the door. "Brix always puts on a good show, Al," he said. "I don't need permission to do that. We'll put on a show and you'll get your money. Or your bank will. Either way, quit worrying. Brix is in town."

* * *

Clay offered to walk Ellie to the Tube station before he headed back for the rescheduled rehearsal, and she was happy to accept, not least as it gave her a little time to ask a few more questions she still had.

"Why do you think someone would go after Cat's sax?" she said, as they turned out of the door into Greek Street. "Do you think it might have anything to do with Al's… issues, with his bank?"

"Yeah, I see what you're saying," Clay said. "Kind of thing someone might do if they wanted to stop the show."

"And stop Al getting his money?"

Clay held out his hands. "Seems like that would be a big deal. I guess we just gotta figure out who it would be a big deal for?"

"Hey – you're that fella from Brix's band!" a voice called up from the pavement. Ellie looked down to see the same scruffy figure on the same corner that she'd seen the night of the show. In the daylight, she could see that he, just like the saxophone he held in his hands, was even more worn and shabby-looking than they'd appeared in the street lights. His face was mottled red with the signs of hard weather and hard liquor, and the saxophone was worn through in places to dull, blackened metal. "You need a sax player?" he said, grinning mischievously as he held up his instrument.

Clay laughed. "Hey, I heard you the other night. You can play, man, you can play. We nearly needed one, I might have called on you."

The man narrowed his eyes. "That Cat walked out on you, has he?"

"Nope," Clay said. "But someone busted his sax."

The man let out a sharp whistle. "Ooh, that's got to hurt," he said. "Hope they catch the blighter."

"I'm sure they will," Ellie said.

"That's the dirtiest crime there is, that is," the man said, holding his instrument to his lips to let out a short flurry of rasping notes. "Nothing worse you can do to a man than to take away his one-and-only. Nothin' worse. I wouldn't give up ol' Brass Bessie here for all the tea in china. Mind, she's old and a bit tired, just like me, but I'd sell me teeth before I sold her. Well, I would if I had any left!" The man let out a wheezing laugh and grinned to confirm he hadn't been lying about his dental work. "Can you spare a poor old musician a couple o' bob?" he said, pushing forward a tattered cloth cap that held a few brass pennies.

Clay reached for his pockets then shrugged as he remembered his stage clothes didn't have any. Ellie opened her purse and pulled out a handful of coins that she threw into the hat.

"Well thank you kindly madam. You are a real lady." He carefully counted the coins and broke into another toothless grin. "Very kind indeed."

"No problem," Ellie said. "I like your playing."

"Thank you, m'am," he said, bowing his head.

As Ellie walked away with a nod of goodbye to Clay the man called out again. "Be sure to pass on my condolences to that Cat of yours," he called. "It's a hard thing to lose a saxophone. Pass on my regards, one musician to the other."

*ELLIE BLAINE 1920s MYSTERIES*

# CHAPTER 9

"SO," Ellie said, "we've got Brix, Clay, Al, Ben, and then… do you mind passing me the sugar tongs, Georgie?"

Georgie frowned as Ellie reached across her to take the silver tongs and place them next to the toast rack that was standing in for the broom-cupboard.

"Who are the tongs?" Georgie said.

"The cleaning lady," Ellie said, resting them among the scattered crumbs below the rack.

"And the toast is…?" Richard asked, raising an eyebrow sharply.

"Eric Prendergast," Ellie said, in a tone that suggested she thought that should have been obvious.

"Why are there two of him?" Richard said.

"What?" Ellie said, glancing back down at the silver rack, which neatly held two rounds of crusty white toast.

"Problem solved," Georgie chirped, reaching over to grab one of the slices and deposit it on her plate. "I hope you don't mind me using Brix Riley to butter spare Eric, do you?" Georgie held up the small butter knife.

"Be my guest," Ellie said, laughing, then shaking her head. "Well, anyway, you get the picture. These are the people who were at the club the night Eric was murdered. And these..." she separated out a small number of utensils and condiments, "these are the ones who were also at the club when Cat's sax was broken. I think it's fair to assume that whoever killed Eric also had something to do with Cat's sax."

"Perhaps," Richard said, now deciding it was time to finish off the last of Eric, before Georgie used up all the marmalade. He took a quick bite, then dabbed at the corner of his mouth with his napkin. "Although I can't see any obvious connection, other than that the two incidents happened in the same place."

"Eric wanted to talk to Cat," Ellie said. "And it sounded like he had something particular he wanted to talk to him about."

"He wanted to talk to Al, too," Georgie said, dropping a sugar cube into her freshly poured tea with the recommissioned tongs, then looking round the elegantly decorated room of the tea house where they were breakfasting, trying to catch the eye of one of the waitresses.

"And Al would appear to have some money issues," Ellie said. "That can be a strong motive for murder."

"But from what you say," Richard said, carefully brushing a stray crumb from his shirt cuff, "Al is desperate for his tour to be a roaring success, so I shouldn't imagine he would want to do anything to hurt his biggest star?"

"No," Ellie said, shaping a frustrated frown and biting her lower lip. "And if Cat was trying to stop Eric from revealing any secrets of his, well that doesn't really fit with his own sax being vandalised."

"And then you have the thing with Cat… " Georgie started. "Oh, to blazes with it, I'm going to call him Louis, I'm afraid I can't get used to calling a grown man 'Cat'."

"You have no problem calling a grown cat 'Mr Madison'," Ellie said with a sly grin.

"That is entirely different," Georgie said.

"Is it?" Richard said.

Georgie sniffed slightly. "Mr Madison and I have known each other for some time, and so it is perfectly acceptable to be familiar with one another. Anyway, my point was going to be that Louis," she sounded the name very deliberately and Richard and Ellie exchanged glances, "refused to go to Paris with the rest of the band. Now why anyone would refuse to go to Paris is beyond me, but particularly a gentleman such as himself who one would think would be very much at home in a city that embraces jazz."

"You think there's a reason he didn't want to go there? Connected to this case?"

Georgie shrugged. "Well, I am just speculating. But this is a chap that no-one seems to know the first thing about until he just turns up one day as an overnight sensation."

"You think he might have a past? In Paris?" Richard said.

"He doesn't sound very French," Ellie said, "not that he speaks much, but when he does he has a pretty strong Chicago accent."

"Well, like I say," Georgie said, waving a dismissive hand. "I'm just speculating."

"Maybe we should start with Eric," Richard said, carefully folding his napkin and placing it neatly on his side plate.

"You're starting to sound like you're getting into this detective lark?" Georgie said, gently nudging his elbow where he sat beside her.

Richard grunted. "I just wonder, if we can't find a motive among the suspects, perhaps we can find one with the victim. Dig a little into what the chap was up to, what kind of a fellow he was?"

Ellie smiled at Richard. "Good thinking. I'll see if I can talk to anyone at his newspaper, see if they know what he was working on."

"And I shall call in some favours among my legal chums," Georgie said brightly. "See if there's any records on any of the chaps from the club. Al

Maguire and that Spats fellow, at the very least, strike me as the sorts of chaps who won't have an untarnished history."

Ellie nodded, as a young, fresh-faced waitress apologetically moved in to show that she was ready to clear the table. Ellie moved aside to let her gather up her plate, while Richard signalled that he was ready to pay the bill.

"It's my treat," he said to Georgie, who he could see was about to insist on paying her part. "I'm afraid I won't take no for an answer."

Georgie made a token protest, well aware that Richard was not one to change his mind. She glanced away as he opened his wallet to take out a crisp note that the waitress accepted with a gentle curtsy, and she caught sight of a face looking in the tea room window. She caught the man's eye and he quickly moved away.

"I say," Georgie said. "Did you see that chap at the window?"

Ellie shook her head.

"Something awfully familiar about him," Georgie said, scratching the back of her head. "Feel like I've seen him before. Rough looking chap."

Richard shrugged. "Someone you've seen in court?" he said, standing up to accept his coat from the waitress before holding the door open to allow Ellie and Georgie out into the street. The road was quiet, in the mid-morning lull, with just the call of newspaper boys and the clatter of hansom cabs and the occasional motorcar on nearby Oxford Street breaking up the cooing of pigeons in the half-empty back streets of Soho that really only came alive at the other end of the day.

"We shall cut through here," Richard said, gesturing to the narrow alley that split Greek Street alongside the wall of the Blue Parakeet. "It's a shortcut to Tottenham Court Road."

As they stepped into the shadow of the alley, Ellie began to wonder if they shouldn't have taken the busier street after all. A figure suddenly stepped out from behind a pile of empty crates, closely followed by another moving from the shadow of a doorway.

"Well well," the first man said. "If it ain't the gallant gent what saved a damsel in distress the other night," the man said. "'Ere, Billy, here's the bloke what dobbed you in."

Georgie turned her head sharply to see the man who had stepped out of the doorway grinning widely and turning a knife in his hand. "I knew I'd seen him before," she said quietly to Ellie, "he's the chap from the club; the one who took Sarah's bag."

Richard looked quickly from one man to the other. "Now we don't want any trouble," he said. "If you have an issue with me let us discuss it like gentlemen, these ladies have no part in it."

"Discuss it like gentlemen?" the first man sneered. "Do you 'ear that, Billy? Pr'aps we should all have a chat about it over a nice cup of tea?"

Georgie coughed loudly. "Gentlemen, we are very well connected members of society and it would not go to your advantage if you were to harm our persons in any way."

The second man stepped forward to tilt his head close to Georgie's. He grinned, showing an uneven row of yellowing teeth. "Well la-di-da," he smirked. "Listen to the well-connected lady. Well, if you are so well-connected I imagine you can afford to help out those of us who don't have the fortune of birth, can't you?"

The man lifted his knife to show Georgie, and she instinctively pulled her head back.

"Do as the chap says," Richard said to Georgie, nodding towards the man. "I have a little money on me," he said to the thief. "You can take that and be damned, but there is no need to harm anyone. Take what you wish and we shall be on our way."

The first man gestured to Richard to open his coat, which he did – handing the man his wallet. Georgie scowled as she emptied her clutch bag and shuddered as the man with the knife roughly unclasped her pearl necklace.

Ellie offered up the few coins she had in her bag, as well as a silver compact Georgie had given her for her birthday.

"Right, you've got what you wanted, now I suggest you let us on our way," Richard said firmly.

"'Ang on," the first man said, pointing at Ellie's arm. "What's that?"

Ellie shook her head. "What?"

"On your wrist, show me!" the man barked. Ellie closed her eyes and turned her hand over.

"Now that is a pretty looking watch," the knife-carrier said, whistling through his broken teeth. "Bit big for a little lady like you, ain't it? I'll have that, thank you very much." The man held out his left hand, still clutching the knife in the other.

Ellie shook her head. "No, I'm sorry. I can't give you that."

"Oh, I think you can," the man said, showing the knife to the side Ellie's left cheek. "If you want to keep that pretty face of yours looking the way it does."

"For pity's sake, man!" Richard barked. "It was a gift from her late fiance, it's all she has left of him. Let her be, here take mine, it is worth far more." Richard reached into the inside pocket of his jacket to draw out a gold half-hunter pocket watch and hand it to the man.

"Ta," the man smirked, pocketing the watch. "I'll take this and I'll take the lady's watch as well, if you don't mind."

Richard's brow darkened, before suddenly brightening in an instant. "Oh, I say! Just in the nick of time, a London bobby! Officer, we are being robbed!"

The two men turned their heads suddenly back down the alley to where Richard was eagerly calling. The alley was as empty as ever ahead of them, and the knife man turned back angrily.

"What are you playing at, you—"

Faster than Ellie could blink, or the man could move his head, Richard's arm swung up in a graceful arc to bring a clenched fist firmly into the man's jaw, knocking him almost upwards from the ground before he fell backwards in a dazed heap on the dirty alley floor. The knife skittered from his hand as he fell, and landed between Ellie and Georgie, who quickly covered it with her foot as the other would-be mugger watched its flight.

Richard rubbed his hand then carefully rolled up his sleeves to raise his fists at the first man. "Now, I strongly suggest you hand back that which you have taken and then you apologise to these ladies," he said. The man looked sharply between Richard, Ellie and Georgie before suddenly throwing down his spoils next to his stunned companion and sprinting away down the darkened alley and back towards the open streets.

"Richard!" Georgie said, a note of incredulity in her voice. "I would never have thought—"

"Thought what? That I might know how to land a decent uppercut? A gentleman must be versed in the sweet science of pugilism," he said. "It's an absolutely necessary part of a proper English education."

Ellie looked baffled.

"He learned to fight in school," Georgie said dryly.

"So did I," Ellie said, rubbing her own chin in sympathy with the fallen thief. "But I never landed one like that."

Richard shrugged. "I simply couldn't let him take my dear brother's watch. Your watch," he said, nodding down to Ellie's wrist. "I'm afraid there comes a point where one must make a stand."

"Thank you, Richard," Ellie said, smiling and turning the watch around her wrist. "I owe you one."

"You owe me nothing," Richard said. "I only did what was necessary."

"Well," Georgie said, "you did it rather well. And timed it well too – look. A little late, but they've arrived after all."

Georgie pointed back down the alleyway in the direction they had entered it. A tall figure dressed in a blue-black greatcoat and helmet was walking cautiously towards them.

"Everything alright, sir?" the policeman said.

"It is now," Richard said, pointing down to the sprawled figure who was just starting to shake himself back into consciousness on the floor in front of him. "I suspect you know this chap?"

The officer looked down. "Oh, we know him alright. Billy Higgins, what the devil have you been up to now?"

# CHAPTER 10

BILLY Higgins had been hauled away protesting his innocence loudly; and rather unconvincingly under the circumstances, Ellie observed. Richard, after a little fussing from Georgie who insisted he took a restorative drink at the Flying Horse on Oxford Street, had caught the Tube back to his town house in Knightsbridge to tend to his bruised hand and finish his newspaper, which he insisted was the proper way to 'settle one's humour'.

"Right," Ellie said to Georgie as the doors of Richard's carriage were pulled closed and his face had disappeared behind the paper walls of that day's Times. "Where is it we need to go?"

"Fleet Street, darling," Georgie said. "All the newspapers fit to read, and many that aren't, will be there; you can practically smell the ink as you walk down the road. Come along, it's just a short hop from here."

* * *

As they came up the steps from Temple Station, Ellie realised Georgie hadn't been entirely exaggerating about the smell of ink. The street buzzed with activity: piles of newsprint stacked for delivery or being bundled off by black-fingered delivery boys; reporters and photographers rushing to, or back from, whatever event was going to be making the first editions of the next day's news; hustle and bustle and noise ripe with scandal, gossip and speculation. The road was lined with bold signs too, hung high above the doors of the tall buildings that ran down either side, bright colours proudly telling which of the many publications owned which particular stretch of Fleet Street.

"That's the one," Georgie said, nodding at a heavy royal-blue and white board that hung from a gallows-like bracket above the lintel of one of the smaller buildings. "London Evening Post – dreadful rag really – but that's where the unfortunate Mr Prendergast worked."

Ellie wasn't sure how much more they would find out from their visit to the dead man's former office; she was certain the police would have already been and taken as much information as was likely to be available, but there was little else to go on at the moment and she was a firm believer in 'if you don't ask, you don't get'. However, the first person they would have to ask was the short, rheumy-eyed doorman on reception, and it appeared all they were going to get this time was the cold-shoulder.

"Sorry ladies; but you can't come in here, I'm afriad. If you want to talk to someone on the news desk, they are all a little busy with today's deadlines. So unless you have some scoop for them that means we have to stop the presses right now, I suggest you make an appointment or write a letter like anyone else. We are a working newspaper office, not a public lobby."

Georgie stepped forward, smiling sweetly, so Ellie knew she would be up to something. "My dear fellow," she said, as gently as she could, which was never quite gentle enough to hide the certainty in her voice that she was about to get what she wanted. "I wonder if perhaps, before you send us on our way, you might pick up that telephone of yours on the desk there and allow me to speak to Lord Farnley?"

"Lord Farnley?" the doorman said. "*The* Lord Farnley?"

"The same," Georgie said. "I believe he still owns this esteemed publication?"

"Yes," the doorman said, looking more puzzled than ever. "But what—?"

"If you could tell him Georgina Parr wishes to talk to him; I'm quite sure he remembers me from that delightful party in Rochester, where he was being the most entertaining company for the bishop's charming twin daughters. He's sure to–"

"Georgie," the voice came from behind them, in a particular resigned-but-accepting tone Ellie was now sure people reserved solely for speaking her friend's name. "I'm sure we don't need to bother Lord Farnley. What can I help you with? Come on in."

The man, dressed in a just-too-tight tweed jacket and with the stain of ink seemingly permanently tattooed into the rough lines of his right hand, put out a hand to usher Ellie and Georgie into a small, windowless office hung with printed papers in various states of yellowing. On the desk, a faded brass sign faintly read: 'Harvey Barnes: Editor'.

"Harvey, how delightful. Thank you so much. It's been far too long, how are you doing? Still running the show at London's most insightful newspaper, I see. How's – oh I do beg your pardon, I've forgotten the name of your delightful wife?"

Harvey gave a knowing look. "Linda is doing just fine, and I'm well, and I'm sure you haven't come here for small talk, Georgie, so let's cut to the chase. I've got tight deadlines to meet so I can't give you long. You after some dirt for one of your clients? Need to get someone off the hook again?"

Georgie coloured deeply, glancing awkwardly at Ellie. "Of course not!" she snapped, her expression of innocence only a little more convincing than Billy Higgins' had been earlier..

"I'm not sure what you are suggesting, but I would never resort to such unethical behaviour. I am a strict adherent to both the letter and spirit of the law."

Harvey's eyebrows had now risen so high Ellie imagined they might catch up with what was left of his balding crown. "Of course you are. So what is it you need?"

Ellie stepped in, suddenly aware that Georgie – for the first time she could recall – seemed lost for words. "We're trying to find out a little more about poor Mr Prendergast," she said. "We think we might be able to help get to the bottom of what happened."

Harvey shook his head sorrowfully. "Poor old Eric," he said. "He was a good reporter. Nasty business, that."

"Do you know what he might have been working on, before he was…"

"Strangled?" Harvey said, finishing the sentence for Ellie. "No – well, I do, but it was nothing special, nothing I could imagine him getting killed for. Just music reviews and some minor society gossip. Eric fancied himself an investigative reporter, but music and society news was what he was best at. He had a good way with words."

"Might he have been trying to investigate something?" Georgie said, now fully recomposed at last.

"Like what?" Harvey said.

"Well, if he fancied himself an investigative reporter, might he have been – you know – investigating?"

Harvey shrugged. "He was always pushing to work in hard news, that was his dream. But I'm not aware that he had anything going on. If he did, he certainly never told me."

"Could he have left any notes here?" Ellie said. "Anything we could look at?"

Harvey shook his head. "Police took all that, and asked all the same questions you are asking," he said. "I couldn't help them much, and I'm not sure I can do any better for you either. Sorry."

Georgie frowned. "Well, then we're sorry for bothering you. We shall bid you good-day and let you get back to your deadlines."

Harvey gave a faint smile and stood as Georgie and Ellie got up from their seats. "I'm sorry I couldn't be more help."

"That's quite alright," Georgie said, trying the door handle ahead of Ellie, "we just thought we might–"

"Oh wait," Harvey said suddenly, holding up a finger. "There might be something; not sure what use it will be, but it's here somewhere." He started to flip up the jumbled pile of double-page spreads that covered the table-top of the cluttered office, his hand stopping suddenly at a small bundle of envelopes. He picked the bundle up and handed it to Georgie. "These came this morning – after the police left."

Georgie turned the bundle in her hand, flicking quickly through it to check the writing on each letter. "These are all for Eric?" she said.

"They are," Harvey said, carefully putting the news spreads back in order. "They'll mostly be from theatre promoters begging Eric to write about them, or else society figures begging him not to write about them."

Ellie let out a laugh. "Not all of them though?"

"No," Harvey said, now gesturing the way out of the door with the impression of a man who was in a hurry to get back to work that wouldn't wait for him. "You might want to look at the top one. I read it, but it means nothing to me. You might understand it better."

"Who's it from?" Georgie said.

"It's from Eric," Harvey said. "Must have mailed it to himself here before he died."

Georgie and Ellie looked quickly at each other, then stepped aside as Harvey politely but firmly stepped between them. "I've got to get back to work,' he said. "Let me know if you make head or tail of it, and good luck."

\* \* \*

"I can see what Harvey meant," Georgie said. "It doesn't make a lot of sense – I'm sure all these names and numbers meant something to Eric, but whatever that was I'm afraid he's taken that with him."

Ellie turned to paper over again. The envelope had contained a single sheet of writing on letter-headed paper from an address in Epping, and little in it except the names of several towns and people and a series of numbers.

"Birmingham 1784, Manchester 1532, Bradford 749…" Ellie read, shaking her head. "Train numbers maybe?"

Georgie shrugged. "No idea. And what about these long numbers?"

"They could be anything," Ellie said, checking off the numbers with her index finger. "One's what? One, two, three - 16 digits long. The other's a bit shorter, four letters and six digits. Could be anything. Safe combinations? Secret code?"

"What about this bit," Georgie said, tapping her finger half way down the sheet of paper Ellie held out in front of her. *"Who are the names?"*

Ellie scanned the letter again, squinting to make sense of the small, scrawly handwriting. "It's like he says, I think, it's a list of names."

"Hmm," Georgie puffed. "Terrible writing., I need my glasses."

Ellie pulled the paper in closer to her gaze. "I can probably read it, let me have a look." She held the paper carefully between thumb and forefinger, putting it down into the light that fell on Georgie's kitchen table from the high roof window. "It is pretty messy writing," she said, "like it was written quickly."

"Like he was in a hurry?" Georgie said.

"Possibly," Ellie said. "It's just names; I don't – oh, wait! Oh!"

Ellie's mouth was open now as she squinted again at the tiny writing, as if to confirm to herself what she'd seen.

"What is it," Georgie said, holding out her hand for the paper, fumbling on her reading glasses.

"There's this first name: Lloyd? Floyd? It doesn't mean much to me, but look at the list just below it. There's a name on there," Ellie said. "Towards the bottom. See if you can recognise it."

Georgie scanned quickly down the list of names, squinting hard to make out the small letters. "Mmm, 'Tom something'," she said, "Pat – Bloop, does that say?"

"Bloom, I think," Ellie said.

"Pat Bloom," Georgie confirmed. "Yes, so-and-so, such-and-such. Where's this– oh! Oh, yes I see. Well bless my soul."

"Bit of a coincidence, wouldn't you say?" Ellie said, smiling.

"Well, yes. More than a coincidence I'll be bound."

Ellie nodded. "Yep," she said. "Twice might be a coincidence, but I make this the third time in the last few days our paths have crossed with Mr Billy Higgins."

# CHAPTER 11

"I TOLD you before, love, this is not something for a young lady to be getting involved in. These aren't nice people."

Ellie ignored the comment, holding back the urge to point out they'd already had a knife pulled on them – twice – by Billy, so she'd worked out he wasn't a boy scout. Instead she smiled as politely as she could. "I have dealt with worse," she said. "And besides, you've got him cuffed and guarded, I don't suppose he can do me much harm from that position."

Rex Kinkaid shook his head. "It's completely out of the question, it's a matter for the police, not amateurs. We can't have just anyone off the street waltzing into a cell to question suspects."

Richard coughed loudly. "I'm not sure what harm it would do," he said, carefully folding back the soft leather of a wallet he had pulled from his jacket pocket, "to ask a few simple questions; with your permission and in your presence, naturally. Here, perhaps if it helps this could cover the cost of any… refreshments we might partake of during our meeting. I should hate to see the station kitty depleted by our presence."

DI Kinkaid looked down at the small bundle of notes Richard handed him. He went to speak, then checked the notes again and tucked them into his back pocket, looking over his shoulder quickly as he did. "Well, the kitty is a little low at the moment," he said, clearing his throat. "Ok – you can see him. Five minutes, no more. And I come in with you."

"Naturally," Richard said. "We should be quite lost in there without professional guidance."

Ellie fought back a smile as she followed DI Kinkaid through a heavy iron-bound door into a narrow corridor lined with a row of more doors, even sturdier than the first, painted in uniform military grey with small, barred windows to the top of each. The inspector flicked through a bundle of keys to find the right one then turned it noisily in the lock and heaved at the door to push it open.

"Wakey wakey sunshine!" DI Kinkaid barked. "You have visitors, Billy boy."

Billy, was laid out on his back on a narrow, thin-mattressed bed covered in bedding long past the point where any amount of starch and bleach could flush out its dirty grey. He sat up, muttering complaints as if he was a hotel guest who'd got his wake-up call half an hour too early.

"What do you want now?" he growled in a thick East London accent. "I was just– bleedin' 'ell! What's he doing here?"

Billy Higgins sat up sharply, jabbing a finger in the direction of Richard and rubbing his still-swollen jaw with the other hand. "Has he come to duff me up again?" Billy said, backing into the corner of his bed. "I've got rights, you know. I shall talk to my lawyer."

"If you had a lawyer," DI Kinkaid said, "I suspect he'd take Lord Melmersby's side in the fight. But don't worry, his lordship is only here to ask you a few questions."

Billy swung his legs over the side of his bed, still holding his face. "I ain't answering no questions. I ain't sayin' nuffin'. I ain't no snitch."

Ellie took the only chair in the room and turned it to sit down and face Billy. "It's alright, it's nothing to do with what happened to us in the alley, we're just trying to put together some loose ends in another matter."

Billy narrowed his eyes suspiciously. "What other matter?"

"The murder of Eric Prendergast," Richard said.

"Now 'ang on!" Billy said, eyes wide and glancing over to where DI Kinkaid stood, looking just as startled by the revelation as the prisoner was.

"I ain't no angel but I ain't no murderer neither. I didn't do nuffin' to no Eric Prenderwhatsit. I never even heard of the bloke. I ain't never murdered no-one."

"No one thinks you did," Ellie said. "But it seems he knew you."

"Is there something we should know, Miss Blaine?" DI Kinkaid said, tapping urgently on the palm of his hand with the large cell key. "Information of this sort needs to come to us. You do appreciate the seriousness of this case, I presume?"

"Of course," Ellie said, as sincerely as she could. "I shall give you all the information we have once we've finished with Billy here."

"I told you," Billie said, "I don't know nuffin' and even if I did I wouldn't tell ya."

"I see," Ellie said. "That's a bit of a problem. Because we have a crime to solve and without evidence we won't be able to solve it. A bit like your case, I suppose?"

"What you mean?" Billie said, squinting.

"Yes," DI Kinkaid said. "What exactly do you mean?"

Ellie smiled. "I mean, if, for instance, Richard and I decided that we didn't really see anything in the alleyway, and that it was all an unfortunate misunderstanding – well, I suppose there wouldn't be enough evidence to see you convicted. What was it the inspector said you were looking at? Three years?"

"Now hold on!" DI Kinkaid barked. "This is a serious matter, you can't—"

Billy stopped his head for a minute, a puzzled look flashing briefly across his ferret-like face before being quickly replaced by a broad, gap-toothed grin. "I suppose you're right," he said. "In that case I shall talk to you – but not with 'im in the room."

Billy pointed at DI Kinkaid who was already shaking his head and now shook it harder, his bundle of keys rattling in time to his movement.

"Not a chance," he said. "You shall all have to leave, this has gone far enough."

Ellie stood. "Give us five minutes," she said. "I think there's a connection here to Eric's murder. If I learn anything I swear you will be the first to know. It's got to be worth letting Billy here go, if it leads to us finding Eric's killer?"

DI Kinkaid shook his head again. "I knew you was trouble the moment I saw you," he said, then sighed deeply. "Very well. Five minutes. And if I find out you learned anything that you don't tell me I shall have you arrested for obstruction, do you understand?"

"Of course," Ellie said. "I will hand myself in and put the cuffs on myself! Thank you."

"I must be mad," DI Kinkaid muttered to himself as he let himself out of the door and shut it firmly behind him. "Five minutes!" He shouted through the small barred window.

"Well done," Billy said, nodding towards the door. "He's been a right pain in—"

"Eric Prendergast was a reporter, Billy," Ellie said, sitting down again opposite him. "He was murdered in the Blue Parakeet, the same night you got escorted out for trying to steal a handbag."

Billy coloured deeply and glared at Richard. "Man's got to make a livin' somehow," he said, rubbing his wrists. "But I already told you, I don't know no reporter and I didn't murder no-one."

"I know you didn't," Ellie said. "But Eric seemed to know who you were. At least he knew your name – here." Ellie pulled the letter out of her purse and handed it to Billy, who held up his hand to stop her.

"Sorry miss," he said. "I… well I ain't much for readin' and so on."

"There's some names on the paper," Ellie said, taking it back and holding it up to the thin light that came through the deep-set cell window. "Yours is on there, so is…" she squinted at the tiny handwriting, "Someone called Lloyd? Someone–"

"Don't know no Lloyd," Billy grunted.

"How about Tom O'Neill, Pat Bloom, Jack… I can't read that one."

"Jack Lymton," Billy said confidently.

"Oh yes, Lymton…" Ellie started, "how did you know that?"

"I know them lot. Pals of mine," Billy said.

"You mean gang members," Richard said.

"No idea what you are talkin' about, guvn'r," Billy said, giving a deep sniff. "Old pals we are, met in Sunday School. Good as gold those boys are."

Ellie shook her head, trying to hold back a smile. "Did they go to the Blue Parakeet with you?"

"Matter of fact, they did," Billy said. "We had a few pals there that night, so we did. Been there a couple of times now, and it's always a real good night."

"Big jazz fan are you?" Richard said dryly.

"Well, I don't really have what you'd call a musical ear," Billy said, grinning. "But I do enjoy the atmosphere, it's very – stimulating."

Richard folded his arms sharply. "You mean you can sell things you shouldn't be selling to people with more money than sense. Do you realise the harm that–"

Ellie turned her head to give Richard a look that stopped him mid-flow, and he crossed his arms more tightly and let out a sharp snort.

"Did any of your friends talk to anyone that night? Someone asking them questions, maybe?"

Billy scratched his head. "Yeah," he said after a moment's reflection. "Not that night though, the night before. Pat was talking to some geezer for quite a while – think the bloke was buying him drinks. Funny sort of behaviour, if you ask me, but you know these jazz clubs…"

"What did he look like, this…bloke?"

Billy shrugged. "Thin, red hair, bit dopey looking."

"Eric," Ellie said, turning to Richard, who unfolded his arms and nodded. "Do you know what they were talking about?"

Billy sat up taller on the small bed. "Not really, think Pat said something like he was trying to find out who we knew in the club. I thought he might be police, you know, but Pat said he was sure he wasn't, and Pat's usually good like that."

"I have a question," Richard said, raising his hand slightly. "Tickets for Brix's show at the Blue Parakeet are, by all accounts, like gold-dust. So how on earth did you and your… pals, get tickets for the second night of the show?"

"First night too," Billy said. "Like I said. As many nights as we like, really."

"Sorry?" Ellie said. "You get free tickets to the Blue Parakeet? Who from?"

Billy puffed out his cheeks. "If I knew, I probably shouldn't tell you. But the truth is, I don't 'ave a clue. Apparently some bloke come to see us in our manor, offered us a whole lot of tickets to the Blue Parakeet. We could 'ave s many as we want, he said."

"Why?" Richard said. "What on earth—"

"He said we was to dress up posh as we could, Sunday best – even gave us a few bob for shoes, just second-hand, mind. Oh, and he said we wasn't to say nuffin' about it to anyone. Which I suppose I just done, but I didn't make no promises."

"Do you know who this man was?" Richard said.

Billy shook his head. "No idea, guv. Never seen him before. None of us knew him. Small bloke, kind of ordinary looking. Nothing out of the ordinary, 'cept his givin' us stuff without us asking; it doesn't usually 'appen like that."

"Thank you," Ellie said. "You've been very helpful."

"Not a problem, miss," Billy said. "And I take it our arrangement still stands? You didn't see nuffin' in the alley and it was all, like you said, a big misunderstanding?"

"Absolutely,' Ellie said. "You have my word."

"What about 'im?" Billy said, cautiously throwing a glance at Richard, "'ave I got your word too?"

Richard flared his nostrils and looked down his long, aquiline nose at Billy. "Do I have your word I shan't have a knife pulled on me again?"

Billy nodded briskly. "You do, guvn'r. In fact I'll go one better. Now, I am not in any sort of gang, you understand, but I know a few blokes who are, and apparently we… they… have a kind of secret code, to keep people we… they… do business with safe."

"Secret code?" Richard said, suspiciously.

"That's right. If you get in trouble with one of the wrong sorts; well, you just say the word and they'll know to leave you alone."

"And can you tell me that word?" Richard said.

"If I have yours that you won't press any charges?"

"You do," Richard said firmly.

"Thank you, guvn'r," Billy said. "Squeaky Weasel."

"Squeaky what?" Richard said, staring blankly at Billy. "What on earth are you blathering on about?"

"Squeaky Weasel," Billy said emphatically. "That's the words. To keep you safe on the street. Well, that's the words this month. They change, you see, so as they can't be used by those what don't have permission. But you've got at least two weeks left with Squeaky Weasel."

"Squeaky Weasel?" Richard repeated back, shaking his head. "Well, I'll be blown."

\* \* \*

"So, I suppose the question is," Ellie said, as she and Richard shuffled down the steep steps of Charing Cross Tube Station in the crush of rush hour traffic, "why on earth would someone give tickets to the hottest show in town to a gang of street thieves?"

Richard grunted an apology as a dour-faced man bumped past him on the stairs, clutching a folded up umbrella to his chest and clearly in more of a hurry than he was. "I can only... sorry!" he called out again to a freckle-faced nanny and her young charge whose way he blocked as he turned to better hear Ellie over the din. "I can only assume they meant to cause trouble," he said.

They reached the bottom of the stairs and moved aside to a quiet, inset arch in the wall, letting the heavy flow of busy commuters rush past them.

"They certainly did that," Ellie said. "No wonder so many people left after the police were called on Billy. Half the club must have been his 'pals'."

Richard shook his head. "Louis' saxophone; wild gangs roaming free – it seems someone is determined to cause problems for this particular show."

"If Al is in trouble financially," Ellie said, "this could finish him, wouldn't you think? Who would gain from that?"

Richard shrugged. "That Spats fellow?" he said. "Rival club manager and whatnot?"

Ellie shook her head. "Al said it was a friendly rivalry, and they seemed friendly enough from what I saw of them."

"Louis then?" Richard said. "Broke his own sax to draw attention away from Eric's death."

"He seemed genuinely upset," she said. "I can't believe he broke the sax, even if he had anything to do with Eric. But if someone is trying to wreck the show, there is something that worries me."

"What's that?" Richard said, checking the traffic of people had slowed down so they could step back out of the alcove.

"They haven't succeeded."

"That's a good thing, isn't it?" Richard said.

"So far," Ellie said. "But whoever they are is pretty determined, and ruthless. I think we haven't seen the last of their scheme yet, and that means no-one at the club is safe."

*ELLIE BLAINE 1920s MYSTERIES*

# CHAPTER 12

"WELL I have to say, this is certainly an upgrade," Sarah said, nodding towards the end of their table that was almost close enough to the stage to reach out and touch it. "I daresay we have the best seats in the house."

Ellie raised her glass in affirmation. "Al said he owed it us, after what happened last time. Compliments of the club."

"Bravo Richard," Sarah beamed. "The dashing hero is duly rewarded." She grabbed Richard's hand across the table and he did his best not let his expression move from its usual neutral setting.

"Yes," Georgie said, sipping carefully at the edge of a wide, and very full, martini glass, "well done old chap. Perhaps they could throw in some complimentary drinks as well; after all, it was a terrible inconvenience."

Ellie laughed. They certainly had a good view of the stage this time, and she had a good view of the room, which she was watching even more closely. Knowing what she did now, it was easier to pick out the members of the crowd who hadn't paid for their tickets – slightly ill-fitting suits, harder faces that didn't look quite so much as if they were used to long lunches. Whoever was paying for their tickets, they were still up to their tricks, it seemed, and she hoped there wouldn't be any more trouble tonight – not least because she wanted to watch Spats a little more closely. The rival club owner was sitting on the adjoining table and laughing a little too loudly at his own jokes that he was sharing with the two young women sitting either side of him. The chance to revisit the club was too good an opportunity to turn down, and not just for the music.

"Oh, show's about to start!" Liz said as the lights dimmed and Al stepped out from the stage wing to a polite ripple of applause and a few hollered cheers from the men in baggy suits. Al looked nervous, Ellie thought, sweating even more than usual and fiddling with his fingers as he pulled aside the curtain to reveal the band already in their places. The applause grew, and Cat raised his new sax to his lips to spin up a cascade of notes as Ben took up the beat.

"Doesn't seem to have affected him," Liz said, nodding at Cat, "losing his sax like that. Sounds simply divine."

Ellie nodded. He was certainly as good as everyone said he was, and, if anything, playing better than she'd heard him the last time, as the band ran through a string of high-tempo, bluesy tunes that had half the audience up on their feet. Sarah had been subtly hinting at Richard stepping out on the dancefloor, but he had put her off by moving the conversation on as quickly as he could, or claiming the music was too loud for him to hear what she was saying. But now the band moved onto a slower song and she saw an opportunity.

"Ellie, darling," she said, beaming a practiced smile. "Could you persuade this stubborn lord of yours to take a turn on the dancefloor with me, I am getting absolutely nowhere."

Richard frowned and Ellie winked at him, which deepened the furrows of his brow further. "Come on Richard, I'm sure this one isn't too scandalous for you."

Richard's face blanched a little at the memory of the last time he and Ellie had been on the dancefloor, at Lady Danvers ball, but Ellie pulled at his sleeve to shake out the unwanted memory. "Go on!" she said, "you know you'd probably enjoy yourself if you let your hair down a little. Be a bit more spontaneous – you might find it's fun."

Richard coughed slightly. "I'm not really the spontaneous sort, Ellie, as you know."

"I do know," she said, raising an eyebrow, "which is why I'm trying to get you to try something different. There's a free spirit in there somewhere, let's get it out!"

Richard turned the corner of his mouth questioningly, then puffed out his cheeks. "Alright," he said. "Dash it, let's try it your way. Would you care to accompany me onto the dancefloor, Miss Blaine."

Richard stood up smartly and held his arm out for Ellie. Sarah glared quickly at Ellie, then stood up to move across her and put her arm through Richard's. "I believe my name was the first on the card," she said, with a rigid smile. "Shall we, Lord Melmersby?"

Richard looked at Ellie, who shrugged. "It was the lady's request," she said, with her best impression of a proper English lady.

Richard held out his free hand to Sarah in acceptance. "Very well, I should be delighted."

Georgie ordered another round of drinks from the waiter, then nudged Ellie's arm to draw her attention, which had wandered to the stage, back out to Richard and Sarah on the dancefloor. "Poor Richard," she said, "I don't think he stands a chance. Sarah is quite used to getting whatever she wants and our dear friend is a lamb to the slaughter!"

Sarah was holding Richard's waist a little more tightly, and a little closer, than was strictly necessary for the practiced steps they performed, and trying her best to hold his increasingly self-conscious gaze. Ellie turned a subtle smile. "He's being spontaneous after all, but knowing Richard, I expect he has weighed up the risk of that," she laughed.

The music stopped and the band took their bow for the interval. Richard excused himself swiftly before disappearing to the cloakrooms, as Sarah returned to the table grinning from ear to ear.

"He's rather nimble on his feet," Sarah said, "I quite refuse to believe he is not a dancer."

"You have succeeded where many a quester has faltered," Georgie said, welcoming her friend back to the seat next to her. "The trick is to repeat the victory; that I have never seen."

Sarah lifted a freshly filled champagne glass. "Well, I'm not one to leave a job unfinished, Georgie. You know that."

Ellie turned to the sound of an excuse-me cough behind her. Clay had stepped down from the stage as Al moved to close the curtain again. "Hi Ellie, mind if I join your table?"

Ellie half-stood to make room for him. "Hey, Clay, of course not. Take a seat."

He nodded in greeting to the rest, then put his long legs under the table and pulled his seat in. "How you all enjoying the show?"

"Wonderful," Liz said. "Better than last time."

Clay smiled. "Thank you," He nodded towards the stage. "How about the Cat? New sax sounding good, right?"

"Absolutely," Georgie said. "Really quite splendid playing."

"Just goes to show," Clay said, "the magic is in the man, not the instrument."

"How's Ben doing?" Ellie said, conscious of the pressure the young drummer must be under with Brix watching him the whole show.

"Ben's doing just fine," Clay said. "Not even Brix can complain." He pulled his chair in even closer to the table and dropped his voice. "Truth is, I think Ben might have had enough of his complaining anyway."

"What do you mean?" Georgie said, feeling the urge to move closer herself into what seemed like it might be a secret worth knowing.

Clay glanced over his shoulder. "Don't tell no-one, but Ben confided in me that he's plannin' to quit the band once the tour is over. He's found it tough. Lookin' for another gig."

"Brix won't like that," Georgie said. "What with Ben's father and so on."

"He won't say nothin' to his pa," Clay said. "He's too scared of Brix, even out of the band. I guess he'll just find some other work and move on."

The sound of the curtain moving again stopped Clay, as Al stepped out from behind it and nodded to him.

"Show's about to start again," Clay said. "I'd best get back up there." He half-stood to leave then turned quickly back. "Say, Ellie. We're only in London for another week. I was wonderin' if, maybe… if it's alright with you…" he scratched the back of his head.

"You were wondering if Ellie would spend some time with you," Georgie said with the confidence Clay had suddenly lost. "And she is, of course, going to say yes."

Ellie frowned at Georgie. "Thanks, Georgie! I can speak for myself."

"So…?" Clay started.

Ellie smiled. "Sure. Why not? Why don't you call over at Georgie's place on Tuesday, I think we don't have much planned for that day."

Clay grinned widely, tipping his head before jumping athletically onto the stage and hauling up his double bass to swing effortlessly into the first song.

Georgie stared Ellie down with a knowing look.

"What?" Ellie said. "I'm only here for a week, so is he, so you can put those eyebrows down now!"

The bass beat picked up as Cat blew through another hot solo, dropping his hands at the end to rapturous applause and signalling to Brix to take up the theme. The band leader stepped forward onto the raised edge of the stage, right above Ellie's table, as Richard returned and took his place.

"He doesn't look well," Richard said as he took his seat. "Brix, I mean. He looks like he may have enjoyed himself a bit too much in the break."

Ellie could see what he meant. All the colour had drained from Brix's face and his brow was drenched in sweat that sparkled in the stage lights.

A flurry of notes rose up from his clarinet, then suddenly faltered; half-blown sounds that fell out of time and ended in a stammer.

"Not well at all," Georgie said, mimicking the raising of a glass to her lips, before swiftly picking up her own to repeat the action for real.

Brix started a line again, this time running out of breath before it finished and leaving notes hanging painfully in the air. Behind him, Ellie could see Ben look up, his face full of surprise which suddenly turned to something she felt looked more like satisfaction at his tormentor's struggle.

Richard frowned. "I'm not sure he's drunk," he said, "he looks terribly—"

His words were knocked out in an instant as Brix dropped his clarinet then suddenly, without warning, toppled forward like a felled tree over the edge of the stage to crash down into their table; scattering glasses and knocking Sarah and Georgie to the floor as table and chairs upturned under his weight.

Screams and shouts rang out from all around the club room, as some ran for the doors and others stood in stunned silence to better see what had happened. Clay rushed forwards to vault off the stage towards his fallen bandleader, while Ben sat in blank bemusement behind his drums, and Cat simply stared at the place where Brix had been standing just moments before.

"What's happened? What is this? Oh no! Oh no, oh no, oh no!" Al had hurried from his seat at stage-side and was holding his head in his hands as he surveyed the wreckage. "Shut the stage down! Everyone out! Everyone out!" he yelled, as he hauled himself hurriedly onto the stage to snatch the curtains closed.

Richard was knelt down among the fallen chairs and had his hand to Brix's neck and his ear laid against his chest. He pulled himself up enough to check Brix's eyes, then shook his head slowly.

"Is he…?" Georgie started.

Richard nodded. "He's dead, yes, I'm afraid he is very much dead."

"Bloody Nora!" a deep voice behind Ellie said, and she turned her head to see Spats standing open-mouthed at the sight of scattered furniture and mayhem. "I should go and see if Al's ok."

Ellie glanced back at Brix, then towards Spats as he moved towards the backstage doors. She looked between the two quickly, then stepped over the remains of shattered glasses to follow Spats, around to the narrow passage between the stage and the back of the room. The heavy loading doors of the club were wide open to the alleyway where they had been robbed by Billy, and Al was standing in the opening, steadying himself on its frame with one hand while drawing heavily on a cigarette with the other. Ellie could see he was shaking.

"Al, mate, are you alright?" Spats said, putting a steadying hand to his back.

"I just needed some fresh air," Al said, turning so Ellie could see his pale face, eyes wet and red.

"I'm ruined, Spats. Ruined. It's over. This is it for me."

Spats stood silently for a moment, then patted Al again on the back. "It'll be alright, pal," he said.

Al turned fully. "Will it? And how, exactly?"

Spats shrugged. "Well, now might not be the time but - if it comes to it - my offer still stands. If that would help you. But it won't come to that, I'm sure. It'll be fine. You'll be fine."

Al shook his head firmly. "No, it's not the time, not the time at all." He began to sob heavily. "This is too much, why did it have to go like this?"

"Can I get you anything," Ellie said softly. "A drink maybe?"

Al looked round suddenly. "Oh, Miss Blaine. I didn't... no, no thank you. I should get back in there, try to clean stuff up. I just..." he shook his head, throwing down the stub of his cigarette into the alley and holding up an excusing hand as he stepped past Ellie and disappeared back towards the dancefloor.

Spats stood looking at Ellie for a moment then forced a weak smile. "Poor old Al," he said, almost apologetically. "And poor old Brix."

"Will Al be ok?" Ellie said.

Spats shook his head. "I told him he would be."

"But...?"

"But," Spats said. "Sorry to say, but I think this might just be the end of the Blue Parakeet."

# CHAPTER 13

"SO, this is quite the coincidence isn't it?" Rex Kinkaid paced the floor in front of the stage, the crunch of broken glass under his feet forcing him to stop and raise his shoe to awkwardly pull a small shard from the leather of his sole. "Same old faces, same place, same crime." He stopped suddenly and flicked the splinter of glass out across the stage. "Except, of course, there are no coincidences. Not when it comes to murder. You!" He jabbed a finger towards Richard, sat awkwardly on Ben's drum stool just below the stage.

"Me?" Richard said, frowning. "I can assure you sir, I had nothing–"

"You weren't here last time, were you?"

Richard shook his head.

Rex curled his lip, seemingly in deep thought for a moment. "But that doesn't mean I rule you out. I'm ruling nothing out. All of you can consider yourselves very much in my line of inquiry. Once we get the toxicology reports I—"

"Cyanide," Richard said firmly.

Rex stared at him for a moment, eyes narrowed. "What?"

"Cyanide. Classic symptoms. The speed of his demise, his colouration, confusion, difficulty breathing, dilated pupils, cardiac arrest. Very typical."

Rex stepped closer to Richard so that he was practically standing over him where he sat. Richard pulled himself up straighter. "You seem to know a lot about cyanide, Lord Melmersby."

"Occupational hazard," he said. "You can't treat people if you don't know what's wrong with them."

"You treat many people for cyanide poisoning do you, sir?"

Richard coloured slightly. "Well, no, I can't say I do. But—"

Rex pulled out his pen to scribble down a few words in his notebook. "No," he said sharply. "I don't suppose you do. Interesting, nonetheless."

Richard coughed. "Well, I should think it is. Cyanide is very quick to act. If he was poisoned with it, it must have happened no later than the interval. And at that point I was visiting the cloakroom and these ladies, and Mr Corliss here, were sitting in very public view at the edge of the stage."

"Clay was with us," Ellie said. "He came to sit at our table."

"Now that is interesting," Rex said, glancing at Spats Corliss, who shrugged in confirmation of Richard's words. "But you boys, you were backstage with him, right?" He waved his hand towards where Louis and Ben sat on the stage edge.

Ben nodded nervously, his freckled face even paler than usual. "We were with him in the dressing room," he said.

"I imagine it must get hot on that stage," Rex said, glancing up at the now empty platform. "Maybe he asked for a drink during the break. Did you give him one?"

Ben shook his head rapidly. "No, of course not. He—"

"He took his usual Wild Turkey," Louis said calmly.

"Wild Turkey?"

"Whiskey," Louis said. "He always takes a shot or two between sets."

Rex looked back to one of the two police officers who stood a few paces behind him, keeping an eye on the group. "Did we have that evidence?" he asked, and one of the officers nodded.

"It weren't that," Louis said, putting his hand down on the stage to push himself up straighter.

"How can you be so sure?" Rex said, scowling.

"Cos I wouldn't be here if it was," Louis said.

"And neither would little Ben. We both took a shot of his whiskey too, he always passes the bottle around."

"Did he drink anything else?" Ellie said. "Water in his whiskey maybe?"

Rex stared at Ellie, hands on his hips. "I ask the questions here, young lady. I think you've probably asked enough already. You're out of depth here, love, so be a good girl and leave it to the professionals."

Ellie bit her lip. There was plenty she wanted to say, but she knew Rex could make it difficult for her to ask the questions she really wanted answers to, so she simply scowled and let him continue.

"Did he drink anything else?" Rex asked Louis, ignoring the scornful snort of laughter Georgie let out.

Louis shook his head. "He takes his whiskey neat. Well he did. He didn't touch nothing else."

Rex turned his back on Louis to address Al, who was swaying slightly in his chair, set a little back from the rest of the group. "What about you? Where were you during the interval?"

Al looked up, his eyes dark-ringed and hollow looking, tired and a little scared, Ellie thought. "I was stood by the stage, the whole time." he said. "I was just there to open and close the curtain and keep an eye on the audience, make sure everyone was happy, buying drinks and so on."

"Could I make a suggestion," Ellie said. "If you're happy to hear an amateur's opinion?"

Rex's lip turned slightly. "I really don't think we need to—"

"It's just that you said if I learned anything from Billy, I should tell you."

Rex sniffed, pulling his neck back and up slightly. "Right. Well, ok then. What is it?"

"I think someone might be trying to ruin Al," she said.

"Ruin Al?" Rex said, turning to stare at the hunched club owner. "What do you mean?"

"The murders, the saxophone – I think they might be connected; that someone is trying to sabotage the tour in order to bankrupt Al. A few of Billy's friends were—"

Rex held up his hand. "Well, yes. Of course. I knew that. Have you only just worked that out for yourself? I was just coming on to that." He coughed, pulling out his notebook again and turning to Al. "So, any idea who might be interested in seeing you ruined?"

Al shook his head mournfully, and Rex turned his glare on Spats Corliss.

"Be awfully good for your business if the Blue Parakeet closed down, wouldn't it?"

Spats stood up sharply. "Now hold on! I'm not sure I like where this is going."

Rex smirked. "No, they usually don't like it; when I ask the awkward questions."

Spats pointed incredulously at his own broad, waistcoated chest. "They? Are you accusing me of—"

"I'm accusing no-one, Mr Corliss" Rex said. "I'm just asking questions." He scribbled a few further notes in his pocket book and Spats sat down heavily, letting out a harsh grunt.

The inspector tucked his book back into his jacket pocket and put his hands together at his waist, nodding to the two officers who returned the gesture and stood back a little. "Now, I think I've asked enough questions for now, but all of you are to stay in London while inquiries continue and–" Clay went to protest and Rex silenced him with a raised finger, "– all of you, that is an order. You are now officially all suspects in a double murder, so stay exactly where I can find you because I can promise you there are going to be a lot more questions yet."

The inspector picked up his long raincoat from the back of one of the chairs and nodded again to the policemen as they walked out together towards the door. At the threshold, Rex turned back suddenly. "Oh, and just one more thing. If you have any ideas about skipping town, or if you think you might even get away with this, just remember this: Rex Kinkaid always gets his man."

"He's rather like Sarah in that respect, then," Georgie whispered to Ellie, with a nod towards Richard. Ellie laughed and the inspector went to speak, then shook his head and turned out of the door.

"We should best get going too," Richard said, standing stiffly from his chair.

"Perhaps you could escort me again?" Sarah said. "I am quite shaken by all that has happened, I might need the attention of a doctor to settle me."

Georgie leaned in again to Ellie's ear. "See what I mean?"

Ellie shook her head. "Come on then, let's get home Georgie. I think all I need is sleep."

"I think there's room for all of us in my car, if you don't mind squeezing up a little," Richard said. "I'm afraid there isn't quite the space for you though, Mr Corliss, I do apologise."

Spats waved a stubby hand. "No problem, squire, I don't live too far that I can't walk it, and the night air will do me good."

Richard nodded and led the group up the short flight of steps and out of the doorway, now darkened with the neon of the club sign extinguished. As they stepped into the cool of the night air, the sound of music drifted down the street, sweet and mellow, almost haunting. Ellie turned her head to see the saxophone man sitting in his usual spot and blowing a familiar melody on his battered sax.

"Is that All By Myself?" Ellie called out to him. "Sounds lovely."

The man put down his sax and nodded. "It is, miss," he said. "Nice tune ain't it?"

The raspiness of his old instrument was gone and the sound was sharper and brighter than she'd heard it before. The man had a half-filled black bottle in front of him that he took a deep draw from. "I heard about old Brix," he said, swallowing a mouthful and raising the bottle in salute. "Nasty business that. I'm playing this one for him."

Ellie walked over to the corner where he sat and pulled out a note from her bag to drop into his hat. "I'm sure he'd appreciate that, Jacques," she said.

"Thank you, miss, and I appreciate the tip. Here, I'll give you one in return."

"A tip?" Ellie said, confused.

"Aye, a tip. Stay away from the Blue Parakeet — it's nothing but trouble, that place. That's my tip." The man put his saxophone up to his lips and his melody caught the night air again in the darkness of the empty street.

# CHAPTER 14

"THE next station stop will be Epping, all passengers for Epping please disembark here."

The train conductor's call snapped Ellie out of her reverie, and she glanced out of the window to see a huddle of rain-coated passengers waiting on the narrow platform of a small red-brick station as the train wheezed to a juddering halt. She wished she'd thought to bring an umbrella, but her head had been full of other thoughts when she came out – questions she hoped she might find some answers to in this small, unremarkable town.

The address on the letter Eric Prendergast had sent himself was as ordinary as the town itself: 9 Jones Street, Epping. If it was Eric's house, then she hoped someone might still be there, and that they might be willing to talk to a strange American woman who turned up out of the blue to ask questions about a murder.

The street was easy enough to find, just a short walk from the station with the help of directions from a friendly porter. A small, well-tended front garden led to a dark green, wooden front door with a heavy brass knocker that Ellie rapped loudly, listening for movement inside the house that would tell her if someone was home. The curtains of a narrow bay window moved slightly, then Ellie heard the patter of footsteps and the rattle of a chain being loosened, as the door opened just a fraction to show the pale, worry-worn face of a woman who looked as if she might be just a little older than Eric was.

"Can I help you, miss?" the woman said, almost apologetically. "I don't buy nothing on the doorstep, if that's what you're hoping for."

Ellie gave a gentle smile. "I'm not here to sell you anything," she said. "I was hoping you might be able to help me."

"Help you?" the woman said, glancing nervously back behind her, as if for back-up that was no longer there.

"My name is Ellie Blaine, I'm – I'm trying to help find out what happened to Eric."

"You with the police?" the woman said.

Ellie shook her head. "I… I knew Eric," she said, trying to look more convincing than her words sounded. "And I work with the police."

The woman opened the door wider, quickly scanning down either side of the street. "Come in," she said sharply. "I'm not sure I can help you any more than I did the police what came here earlier, but come in."

Ellie shook out her wet shoes, scuffing the soles dry on the rough hessian doormat and followed the woman into the house. A small, cramped hallway led off to a single downstairs room, huddled with soft furniture upholstered in garish yellows and blues. The little space left in the room was mostly taken up with open cabinets of colourful trinkets and keepsakes, china kittens, dancing ballerinas, knitted pom-poms and polished horse-brasses. It didn't look much like the home of a hard-bitten reporter.

"Was Eric your—"

"My brother," she said. "Oh, where's my manners? Linda Prendergast," she said, holding out her hand for Ellie to take. Linda shook her hand then subtly wiped it dry on her apron, and Ellie realised just what a sight she must be, soaked from the steady rain that had fallen all along her path to the house.

"Do you mind if I sit down?" Ellie said.

"Of course, be my guest." Linda gestured towards a well-stuffed armchair squeezed into the corner of the room and penned in either side by two large aspidistras. Ellie sat down, sinking into the deep cushion and pushing a large leaf aside to better be able to talk to her host.

"I won't keep you long," she said. "I believe that what happened to your brother might be to do with something he was investigating. I don't suppose he told you anything about a story he might be working on?"

Linda shook her head sadly. "I'm afraid not. He didn't talk too much about his work. He liked to keep it close to his chest, very secretive that way, in case he got scooped, he used to say."

"So nothing in particular, " Ellie said. "Nothing recent?"

"I can only tell you what I told that detective what came here; he was definitely quite excited about something, but he didn't tell my much about it. Just said that he reckoned he'd got a really good story he was working on, said it would make his name, so he did. And he was out and about a lot more, till all hours, working on it."

"Might it have had anything to do with Brix Riley and his band?" Ellie said.

"Brix Riley? Well, I don't know, but he seemed very keen on that band. But then he writes about jazz, you see, as well as the goings-on in society. Very good writer he is, I was always so proud of him." Linda wiped away a tear that was growing before it had time to fall, and Ellie nodded sympathetically.

"Did he tell you anything about the band?"

Linda shrugged. "Not a great deal, no. Except I know he was planning on following them; once they left London. Got tickets to all their shows –

Birmingham, Manchester, Bradford, half a dozen other places too."

Ellie was silent for a second. Of course, the places on his list matched the towns Brix was going to play in. She quietly cursed herself for not working that out before, and reached into her bag to pull out the letter Harvey Barnes had given her.

"Do these numbers mean anything to you?" she asked, showing the letter to Linda, who shook her head.

"Don't mean nothing, sorry."

Ellie folded the letter and slipped it back in her bag. "I am determined to find whoever did this to your brother," she said. "It would be a real help if you could let me see any papers Eric might have left behind, anything to do with his work."

"Police took all of them," Linda said. "Not that there was much, but what there was they took."

Ellie scratched her head. "You don't have anything of his? No notes? Records?"

Linda shrugged. "The only scrap of paper they didn't take was a magazine I found under his mattress when I turned over his room this morning. Not much use to you I don't think, all in French it is."

"French?" Ellie said, suddenly sitting up to perch on the edge of her seat.

"Aye," Linda said. "He went to Paris a few months back. That's not like him, I thought – he usually goes to Margate for his holidays. But he said it was for work, and I said well I jolly well hope they are paying for it. It's not cheap, you know, going to Paris."

"What sort of a magazine?"

Linda coloured slightly. "Well, when I found it under his mattress, I didn't know what it was. What with it being from Paris and everything, well you can imagine what I was thinking. You know what those French are like. But it's alright, I took a look at it and I can't read a word but it seems to be about jazz. He loved his jazz, you know."

"Could I see it, maybe?" Ellie said.

Linda nodded to a small magazine rack sitting just under the smaller of the two aspidistras. "It's right there, where it should be," she said. "A place for everything and everything in its place, that's what I say. It's quite an old tatty thing, I think – date on the front says 1920, so I'm not sure why he would have bought it, I'm sure it's quite out of date now."

"Thank you," Ellie said, flicking quickly through a bundle of knitting magazines and old train timetables to retrieve the magazine, a flimsy publication printed on cheap paper that had caused the ink to run in places.

"Read French, do you?" Linda said, nodding at the paper in Ellie's hands.

"I don't," Ellie said. "But I know someone who does. Do you mind if I borrow this?"

Linda shrugged. "You can keep it. It's no use to me, I don't know nothing of French, nor jazz for that matter."

"Thank you," Ellie said. "You've been a real help."

\* \* \*

"I'm sure I'm missing something," Ellie said as she and Georgie looked over the magazine, spread out on the small kitchen table of Georgie's town house.

"Well, right now we are both missing someone who can understand what's written here," Georgie said. "Typical of Richard to be gallivanting off around town when we need him."

Ellie turned her mouth slightly. "I thought you were keen to see Richard and Sarah getting on?"

"Well, I suppose," Georgie said. "For the pure gossip value at least – oh, don't look at me like that, I know you like gossip as much as I do. You practically live in Mrs Garnet's tea shoppe."

Ellie laughed. "Well, we'll have to wait until he gets back from taking his new friend to dinner before we have either gossip or a translator I guess."

"I shall call Liz," Georgie said. "She speaks French – like a native. Her family have a delightful place in the Loire Valley, they holiday there every Spring. Wait there, I shall telephone her at once."

Ellie helped herself to another Rich Tea biscuit and stared at the magazine again. There were no pictures, just walls of unintelligible text that she imagined might hold a secret – perhaps even one worth killing a man for. Or, it could simply be reviews of obscure French jazz bands; either way, Liz would hopefully uncover it for her.

"Do you mind getting that?" Georgie called out from the atrium where she kept her telephone. "I'm just on hold for the operator."

Ellie turned her head to the sound of an insistent knock on the door. She wondered if it might be Richard after all, seeking refuge from the attentions of Sarah who she was sure must have been the instigator of their dinner date.

Instead, as she opened the door, she saw the stony face of Inspector Kinkaid, clutching a neatly tied bundle of papers.

"Inspector?" Ellie said, surprised. "What brings you here?"

"I was told this is where I could find you," he said, stepping into the room. "Mind if I come in?"

"It seems you're already in," Ellie said. "Can I get you anything?"

The inspector held up a hand, laying the papers down on the table with the other. "No thank you, I'm not staying. I just bought these over for you."

Ellie stared at the stack of documents. "What are they?"

"Eric's papers," the inspector said. "I had a phone call from his sister this afternoon, saying someone had been round asking after them. It seems, as hard as I try, I can't keep you away from this case can I?"

Ellie gave an apologetic grimace. "Well, no. Sorry."

"So, if you are going to be nosing around I suppose you should make yourself useful. We've gone through all of these but there's nothing in there that gives us any clue as to what happened to Eric, or why. I was going to get them sent back to Miss Prendergast, but she reckons you can have them. So there you are. Take a look through them, see what you can find. I don't suppose it will be much, but if it keeps you busy and away from knocking on people's doors or snooping where you're not needed, then it has its purpose."

"Um… thank you, I think," Ellie started.

"Good day to you, miss," the inspector said, putting his hat back on his head as he stepped back through the doorway. "And if you do happen to find anything, tell me first. Understood?"

"Understood," Ellie said, with an exaggerated nod of her head.

The door shut firmly just as Georgie stepped back into the room. "Liz can't make it until tomorrow," she said. "And who was that at the door? Not that busy-body from number 3 again, was it?"

"It was our inspector Kinkaid," Ellie said. "And he brought me Eric's papers." She gestured to the bundle on the table.

Georgie inspected them momentarily, rubbing her chin curiously. "That doesn't seem likethe sort of thing he would do," she said. "I thought he wanted to keep meddling young women out of his work."

Ellie shrugged. "I think he just wants to keep me busy," she said. "Keep me out of mischief."

Georgie pulled her chin sharply into her neck. "Now why on earth would anyone want to do that?" she said. "It is my observation that mischief is the very best place for you. You are never more yourself than when you are right up to your rather elegant neck in it!"

# CHAPTER 15

"WELL, I've got to be honest, it's not what I expected we'd be doing today, but I'll help as much as I can."

After the chaos of Brix's demise at the Blue Parakeet, Ellie had quite forgotten she'd invited Clay over for the day. Not that she minded; not least as Liz was busily scouring the scrappy magazine Eric's sister had given her, and it would be helpful to have someone who understood jazz as well as Liz understood French. Though, at the moment, it seemed neither of them understood the writing in the paper as well as they might.

"Looks like Liz could do with some help, Clay," Ellie said, tipping her head towards her friend, who was standing back from the table on which it was set, with her hands firmly on her hips and shaking her head.

"I mean, half of it is incomprehensible!" Liz puffed, "These French jazz types certainly love their slang. I shall need a jazz dictionary as well as a French one to read all this."

"Has anything caught your eye yet?" Ellie asked hopefully.

"Remind me again what it is I am looking for," Liz said. "I have quite lost track of it."

"I'm not really sure," Ellie said, leaning over to look at the pages again, and just as unable to read a word of it as she was before. "Anything that might have some connection with Brix, or the Cat, I suppose."

"Hmm," Liz said. "Well, we've got a piece here about some chap called Eugene Bullard, seems he was a fighter ace in war, American chap, and now he's quite something on the jazz scene in Paris. That any use?"

"Maybe," Ellie said. "But I don't see a connection other than he's American. Is there anything else?"

"Oh look," Liz said suddenly, jabbing her finger at a small article set at the bottom of the same page. "Looks like someone has left a mark here – do you see?"

Ellie picked up the paper to squint at it. Around the headline she could just make out the faint outline of a circle, made with a pen that must have been running low on ink. She scolded herself for not noticing it before. "That must have been Eric," she said. "What does it say?"

"Thierry Le Magicien Disparaît," Liz said, waving her arm in the air theatrically.

"Something about a magician?" Ellie said, staring blankly.

"Thierry The Magician Disappears," Liz said. "It's a piece about a jazz fellow, sax player by the looks of it. Seems he was very highly thought of."

"Was?"

"He disappeared," Liz said. "As the headline suggests. Didn't turn up for a show, not been seen since. No sign of him anywhere. The article is asking jazz lovers to keep an eye out for him."

"Thierry?"

"Thierry Renault," Liz said. "There's not much else on him, except that he got his nickname for being a bit of a wiz on the sax, apparently."

Ellie turned to Clay, whose face was as blank as her mind felt. "Do you know anything about this 'magician', Clay?"

Clay shook his head. "Tell the truth, I don't know much about French jazz at all. There's a few of our fellas play over there, mostly cats who went over for the war and found they liked the air in Paris. I ain't never heard of no Thierry Renault."

"Gosh, I don't suppose… no," Georgie started, quickly correcting herself.

"Suppose what?" Ellie said.

"Oh, it's nothing." Georgie waved away the comment. "It's just… well, you said how Louis didn't want to go to Paris. You don't suppose it might have had anything to do with this Thierry chap, do you? I mean, why else would that reporter have marked the story?"

"I don't think Cat has ever been to Paris," Clay said. "Not that I know of. Course I don't know much of anything about him, no-one does, but he's never mentioned it at least."

"What are you suggesting?" Liz said, frowning. "That Louis might have bumped off this French jazz fellow?"

"No! Absolutely not!," Georgie protested. "It's just – there was that story about him stealing his saxophone off someone, isn't that right, Clay?"

Clay looked uncomfortable, holding back a scowl. "That's just a story, Georgie. Creates a mystique, you know. I know Cat enough to know he ain't no thief."

"Oh no, of course not!" Georgie said, holding up her hands and waving them frantically. "I'm not suggesting that at all. But perhaps Eric might not be so trusting as I am, you know, maybe he got the wrong end of the stick and all that?"

"Whatever it was, he certainly seems to think it was worth investigating," Ellie said. "And whatever he was investigating was enough to get him killed. We need to see if we can find out any more about this Thierry guy."

"Well if it's obscure jazz musicians you want to know about," Liz said, "I know just the chap you should be talking to. Walter Pickens is your man."

"Walter Pickens?" Ellie said.

"Yes, owns a recorded music boutique, just off Charing Cross Road. If it's jazz, he'll have heard it. His shop is a veritable Aladdin's cave of gramophone records."

"Ok," Ellie said, picking up her bag from where it was slung over the back of a kitchen chair. "What are we waiting for, let's go see Mr Pickens."

\* \* \*

"Thierry… what was it again?"

Walter Pickens' shop certainly lived up to the billing, with records stacked all around so that you had to negotiate a tall, twisting maze of cardboard boxes to find your way to the small shop counter. But whoever Thierry Renault was, it seemed news of his talent, and his disappearance, hadn't reached this side of the Channel just yet.

"Renault," Ellie said. "Thierry Renault. French sax player, would have been in Paris around 1920."

Walter shook his head. "I know quite a few of those French cats," he said, "but I've never heard that name before. You sure you've got it right?"

"Yes," Ellie sighed. "Well, thanks for trying anyway."

"Sorry I couldn't be more helpful," Walter said. "If there's anything else I can help you with, let me know. I've got some new records just off the ship from America, I'll give you a small discount if you buy more than one."

"Thanks, but…" Ellie started.

"Here, how about this one," he said, handing Ellie a blue-labelled record in a pristine sleeve of brown waxed paper. "Eddie Elkins' Orchestra, great band. You'll enjoy this one."

Ellie forced a smile and turned the record in her hand. "Thanks, I'm not sure I–" She stopped suddenly, tracing the label carefully with one finger, before holding it out to Walter. "What's this number, here?"

Walter picked up a pair of half-moon glasses that sat on the counter, squinting at where Ellie was pointing. "That? That's just the catalogue number, for this record. Every record has one."

Ellie looked at the number again, 16 digits. She reached into her handbag and pulled out the folded envelope, drawing Eric's letter out again to put down on the counter in front of Walter. "Is that what this is?" she said, pointing to the 16 digits Eric had written out.

Walter squinted again. "Hmm. Could well be," he said. "Do you want me to look it up for you?"

Ellie's face suddenly brightened. "Yes please, that would be just swell!"

"Be right back," he said, turning to disappear through the narrow doorway behind the counter.

"You think Eric was looking for a record?" Georgie said.

"Looking for, or found," Ellie said. "And whatever that record is, I'm going to bet it has something to do with what happened to him."

"Here you go," Walter said, emerging from the door again with a wide grin on his face and a faded record sleeve in his hand. "Your luck is in after all, I don't suppose anyone has asked for this record in years, I just had it in an old job lot I picked up ages ago. Recorded in 1914, this was. Got to say, you have very obscure taste, what with this and some French fella I've never even heard of."

"Who is it?" Ellie said.

"It's an old vaudeville band, from Chicago, called The Sweet Six. As far as I can see, this is the only record they ever made. I've never listened to it. Do you want me to put it on?"

Ellie nodded enthusiastically and Walter cranked the handle of the old gramophone player that stood on his countertop, carefully dropping the needle onto the record, which started with a heavy crackle that broke into a jaunty blues-tinged melody.

"Bit old-fashioned now," Walter said. "But they sound a decent band."

"Who's the sax player?" Ellie said, nodding at the record as it turned to play the sound of a sharp, staccato solo.

Walter followed the turn of the record label as it span on on the turntable. "Some guy called Amos Jackson, by the look of it," he said. "Again, I don't know much about him."

"The band's from Chicago, you said?" Ellie looked at Clay. "Like The Cat. If Eric was researching Louis, you don't suppose—"

"That ain't Cat," Clay said, shaking his head firmly. "If that's what you're thinking. The guy on that record is a good player, but it ain't The Cat. He's not on the same level as Cat, he's not even on the same planet as Cat. Cat's a genius, this guy's just a steady pro. Nope, that ain't him."

"So why was Eric so interested in this record?" Ellie said. "What possible connection could there be?"

Clay shrugged. "Maybe he just liked vaudeville? It might be nothing to do with his story at all."

Ellie puffed out her cheeks. She was sure there was more to it than Eric's musical taste, but what that was was no clearer now than when she'd first seen the number scrawled on his self-addressed letter.

The sax player in The Sweet Six might not be The Cat, but Louis Luther had something to do with all of this, she was sure of that. Paris, Chicago, mysterious numbers and missing saxophone players: the Cat from Nowhere was caught up in this somehow, and if she was going to find out how, she would need to discover just exactly where Nowhere was, and how the Cat found his way out of there.

# CHAPTER 16

AS she waited outside the gloss-black front door of an elegant Georgian, three-story townhouse it struck Ellie that although she had got to know Richard very well over the last year or so, there was still much about him that remained a mystery. She had never seen his London home before, nor imagined it would be quite so grand, though she supposed she should have done – he was Lord Melmersby after all. He picked his conversations carefully, even now, and they were rarely about himself.

Ellie went to ring the bell again, but now the door opened slowly to reveal a hard-faced woman of a certain age, dressed in an immaculately pressed house dress, with even more precisely sculpted grey hair, ordered into a disciplined bun with a jet-tipped hairpin.

"Good morning, m'am. May I inquire as to your purpose in calling on Lord Melmersby?"

Ellie was taken aback for a second, wondering if she had discovered some unmentioned relative of Richard's, before realising that, of course, he would have a housekeeper in London.

"Good morning," she said, more warmly than the same words had been spoken to her. "I wonder if you could let Richard know that I've called on him; the name's Ellie."

The woman's expression remained as fixed and unmoving as her hair. "Are you acquainted with his Lordship? He isn't in the business of greeting strangers at his door," she said.

Ellie shook her head. It seemed Richard really was practiced in keeping his personal life as neatly tucked away into compartments as he kept his paperwork in the family study. "I'm a friend of Richard's," Ellie said. "I'm sure he'd be happy to see me if you could just inform him."

The woman paused for a moment, straightening out the hem of a sleeve that already looked perfectly straight to Ellie. "I'm afraid Lord Melmersby is not at home."

"Oh," Ellie said. "Do you know where he has gone? It's just that I have some rather important news to share with him."

The woman's face turned even harder than it had been so far, which was quite an achievement,

Ellie thought. "His Lordship was in the company of Miss Sarah Fotheringay last night, and has yet to return. Shall I inform him of your calling?"

"Oh!," Ellie said, lost for words for a second. "Um… no, that's ok. I'm sure I'll catch up with him soon. Thank you. Yes, thank you."

\* \* \*

"Well I say!" Georgie said, her face breaking into a mischievous grin. "How frightfully scandalous. Well, good for him, I say. It's about time he let his hair down."

Ellie shook her head. "It's hardly scandalous; they are both unattached. Just – I'm a bit surprised. It's not like Richard. At least I don't think it is?"

Georgie examined her friend closely, narrowing her eyes as she did. "I say, you're not feeling a little jealous are you?"

Ellie pulled herself up sharply to throw an admonishing look at Georgie. "No! Of course not. Don't be silly. It's just – well, with everything that's been going on I'm just a little worried about him not returning at night." She shrugged. "I suppose I shouldn't be. I guess I did encourage him to be more spontaneous."

"You did, and he seems to have taken your words to heart and now I shall tease him mercilessly over it. Well done you!"

Ellie let out a weak laugh. "I do still need to talk to him about Thierry Renault and that vaudeville record. We should call around again later. In the meantime, do you fancy heading back into Soho? I'd like to catch Clay at the club – I did promise him a day out in London and I'm not sure yesterday counted."

"I can't imagine a better day out than chasing clues for a dastardly murder," Georgie said. "But I'm happy to oblige. Oh, and speaking of clues, I may just have one for you."

"You do?" Ellie said. "What–"

"You're not the only sleuth in town," Georgie said, with a self-satisfied grin. "I told you I would do a little digging in the files and whatnot, and I may just have stumbled across a nugget."

Ellie gave her friend a curious glance. "What kind of nugget?"

"The golden kind," Georgie said. "Also the utterly unprofessional of me to be looking at kind, so let's keep this between ourselves. But anyhow, I was pootling about in the files of an acquaintance of mine who works in conveyancing, property law and such, as I knew Mr Maguire was a client of his. In my defence, he chose to leave me alone in his office, admittedly after I persuaded him to go out and check on his automobile, which I had informed him was receiving undue attention from a group of street urchins. So really, it was his fault to leave confidential documents in full view. Well, by in full view, I mean of course in his filing cabinet, but he hadn't locked it and so–"

Ellie laughed. "Maybe just skip to the nugget?"

"What?" Georgie said. "Oh yes, the nugget. Well, it seems that Mr Maguire really is in a bit of financial bother. He mortgaged his house about nine months ago, to the tune of £10,000, and then barely two months ago he took out a £5,000 loan against the title deeds of his club. Seems that financing this tour really was an expensive business."

"That's a lot of money," Ellie said, turning her mouth in thought.

"It is," Georgie said. "But there's more to this nugget yet. It appears the Blue Parakeet has been in financial difficulty a couple of times in the last four years. Apparently Mr Maguire managed to turn it around both times, but not after almost accepting offers for the club from a perspective purchaser."

"Who was the purchaser?" Ellie said.

"A certain Mr Anthony Corliss," Georgie said. "Better known to us as Spats."

\* \* \*

The Blue Parakeet was rarely open at lunchtime during the week, but there were staff there stocking the bar and cleaning tables, so the door opened to Georgie's knock and the cleaning lady they had seen on the day of Eric's murder ushered them in.

"If you're looking for Mr Clayton," she said. "He's at the back bar, with that friend of yours."

"Friend?" Ellie said, puzzled. "Which one?"

The cleaning lady didn't need to answer; as they turned into the main dancefloor area from the entrance corridor Ellie could see Clay, sat high up on a tall barstool, deep in conversation with Richard.

"Richard!" Ellie called out across the width of the room. "I didn't expect to see you here."

Richard and Clay turned to her call, Clay raising a hand in welcome and Richard nodding respectfully.

"Hi Ellie," Clay said. "You looking for Richard?"

"I was looking for you," Ellie said. "Well, I was looking for both of you, I just didn't expect to find Richard here."

"We were talking about your case," Clay said. "Richard's been doing some detecting of his own."

In the low light of the bar, Richard's face looked tired and drawn. He nursed a large, black coffee and nodded at Clay's words.

"I hear you had a pleasant evening with the beautiful Sarah," Georgie said with a sly grin. "Is that what the coffee is for?"

Richard looked down casually at his cup, then shrugged. "No Georgie. I did have a pleasant evening with Miss Fotheringay, though it ended rather sooner than expected. The coffee is for what I did with the rest of the night."

"Oh," Georgie said, sounding disappointed. "So you and Sarah didn't…?"

Richard raised a sharp eyebrow. "I'm not sure it would be any of your business what Sarah and I did or didn't do. But in answer to your rather inelegant insinuation, no. We didn't. Sarah returned home, and I spent the night in hospital. Or rather, several hospitals."

'Hospital?" Ellie said, sitting down swiftly at the seat beside Richard. "Are you alright? Did anything happen?"

"Well," Richard said, looking at Clay, who nodded slowly in response. "Something did happen, but not to me."

"To who then?"

"Jacques," Clay said, glancing out in the direction of the back door that led to the old street musician's curb-side spot.

"Jacques? Is he alright?"

"Jacques is dead," Richard said flatly.

"Dead?" Georgie gasped. "How?"

"Well," Richard said, pushing himself up on his barstool. "Therein lies a tale. Sarah and I were on Greek Street last night, having just been to dinner at a rather splendid restaurant on Manette Street, and were taking a postprandial constitutional–"

"Post–prandi-what-now?" Ellie frowned.

"He means after-dinner walk," Georgie said. "Richard, do get to the point and talk the King's English, there are normal people here."

Richard scowled at Georgie and continued. "Well, we were just walking along outside here and I saw a lady I recognised from my clinic in the East End. She was laying flowers at the corner of the street, just where Jacques used to play. So, naturally I asked her the purpose of her tribute, and she informed me that the poor gentleman had passed away."

Ellie shook her head. "Did she say how?"

"She said that the official word was that he'd been found dead by a police officer late on Monday night, and that he had succumbed to years of heavy drinking. But the lady I spoke to was adamant that was not the case. She insisted that he was a fellow of stout constitution, despite his unhealthy habit, and that he had not drunk to any excess – at least not by his standards – that night."

"Do you have any ideas on what might have killed him?" Ellie said.

Richard took another sip of coffee, grimacing slightly at its bitterness. "I do – but it was not a simple task finding out. That's where I was all night. I took a tour of London's hospitals, calling in on my various colleagues and acquaintances."

"Why?" Georgie said. "The chap was dead, I don't suppose they could do much for him."

Richard rolled his eyes, not as subtly as he had meant to, and Georgie folded her arms firmly in response. "His body would have been taken to a mortuary at one of the hospitals. As it happens, it turned out he was at London Hospital, which I suppose I should have tried sooner, but it was rather late by the time I got there."

"What did you want with his body?" Ellie asked.

"I wanted to see if he had indeed died in the manner the police described. He was a vagrant, not the sort of chap that anyone would spend any time or consideration on in life or in death, unfortunately. I imagined that they would write off his death without looking too much further into it. I, on the other hand, thought it well worth consideration, particularly with it happening so close to the Blue Parakeet, and all that has gone on there in recent days."

"And did you get your answer?" Ellie said.

Richard cleared his throat. "I did. And I am certain he did not die from the effects of drink."

"Then what did he die of?"

"Poison."

"Poison?" Ellie and Georgie looked at each other.

"Poison," Richard repeated. "More specifically cyanide. And on the same night Brix Riley was murdered in the same way. I am afraid that whoever the killer at the Blue Parakeet is, it appears they have struck again."

*ELLIE BLAINE 1920s MYSTERIES*

# CHAPTER 17

GEORGIE'S kitchen table had long given up any pretense of serving its original function – partly because Georgie never cooked when there were far too many good restaurants in London, and partly because it had now been entirely commissioned as the 'evidence board'; covered completely with notes, scribbles and documents, one of which, Ellie hoped, might give them the breakthrough they were looking for. However, it didn't seem likely the papers Rex Kinkaid had dropped off would be of any use in that department.

"So, have you learned anything?" Georgie said, pacing the floor while Ellie flicked through the last of the thick pile of documents and Clay leaned against one of the kitchen units watching.

"Not a thing," Ellie said. "Other than that Eric liked to shop at Selfridges, but didn't really have the income for it. It's mostly receipts, bills, and final demands. A few snippets of his articles, a letter rejecting his job application at The Times, a couple of old shopping lists, an appointment card for his chiropodist, some old Christmas cards. That's about it. I think Rex really was just trying to keep me occupied."

Georgie puffed out her cheeks and sat down on one of the elegant kitchen chairs that lined her table, dropping her elbows on the table top and her chin into her hands. "What about those ones?" she said, nodding to a bundle of open letters tied neatly with green ribbon and placed on the dresser to the side of the table. "We haven't looked through those."

"Oh, those are mine," Ellie said. "Livvy sent them down from Melmersby for me, I've got to sign off on a couple of things, financial stuff. Apparently its urgent."

Georgie shrugged, sitting a little more upright now. "Perhaps we need to be looking elsewhere? What about the street musician chap? He had nothing to do with the show, so if someone was trying to stop it, why bump him off. Besides which, the show is already over, what with Brix dead. Maybe we've got the motive all wrong?"

"There's a chance the show might still go on," Clay said. "Well, there was but I don't think it's going to happen now."

"Without Brix?" Ellie said. "How?"

"Tommy offered to step in. He said it was the least he could do for old Brix, and besides I think he liked the idea of playing to bigger crowds than he got at Spats' place; looks like the English appetite for jazz don't go no further than the Blue Notes."

"I wouldn't think Cat would appreciate another saxophone player in the band," Georgie said. "I don't know the fellow, but I get the impression he's not one for sharing the limelight."

Clay let out a sharp laugh. "Well, you got that right. No, Tommy would take over on clarinet, step into Brix's shoes."

"I didn't know Tommy played clarinet?" Ellie said.

Clay shrugged. "He started out on clarinet, but didn't make it big until he picked up the sax. Tommy used to say they work pretty much the same but you have to talk to them different – clarinet is like a show pony you gotta talk soft to and sweeten up with sugar, sax is a stubborn mule you gotta holler at to get it to work, but at the end of it they are kinda the same animal. That's what he used to say."

"Would that work? For the show?" Ellie said.

Clay shook his head. "Guess we'll never know, Al straight up turned him down. Said folks would feel cheated if Brix weren't heading his own band; said the audience would never go for it, they'd demand their money back, and it would ruin his reputation more than closing down the show."

"That's a shame," Ellie said. "What happens to you and the rest of the band now?"

"Well, Al's sorted out tickets on a ship out of Southampton next week, which was mighty big of him, I think. Looks like we'll hang around London for a few days then be back on our way. We've got a room at the club till then – we gotta share, but the beds are soft and the room is warm, we've stayed in far worse, believe me."

Ellie gave a nod then turned back to the table to flip through the papers again, a frown of frustration showing itself on her face. "We should get back to this," she said. "There's bound to be something among all this."

"Say, Ellie – maybe you need a break from all that reading," Clay said. "How about we go out and get a coffee, I've found a great spot just down the road from here. Little Italian place. Nearly as good as the coffee back home."

Ellie sighed. She was glad of Clay's company, but it seemed he was getting bored even more quickly than Georgie and this was the third time he'd tried to suggest they take a break. Perhaps he was right, she thought; she certainly wasn't getting anywhere re-reading shopping lists.

"Ok," she said. "But first I just want to brainstorm things one more time."

"Always one more," Georgie said. "Twelfth times a charm, I guess."

Ellie ignored her. "So, let's still assume the motive was to shut down the show. That's my best guess for now. If that's the case, how would Jacques fit into that?"

"Well," Clay said. "I guess he might have seen something. He hangs around by the club at all hours, so maybe he saw someone go in."

"Or out," Ellie said. "That's a good point."

"And he was killed just a short time after Brix," Georgie said. "So that would fit with that. Perhaps the killer slipped out of the club and bumped into Jacques on the corner. He would know he'd been seen, so he sneaked back later to get rid of the only witness."

"Maybe," Ellie said. "Jacques had a bottle when I saw him, perhaps the killer gave it to him, laced with cyanide. Be a simple way to get rid of him."

"Simple, and ghastly," Georgie said. "The poor chap."

"What about the letter – the one Eric sent to himself. Have you found out any more from that?" Clay asked.

"Just that the towns mentioned in it are the ones your band was meant to be playing in. I still have no idea what the numbers next to them mean, nor the other long number."

"And the names?" Georgie said, flipping over one of the useless documents idly. "Those are all Billy's friends I take it? Perhaps we should talk to some of them?"

"I've no idea how to find them," Ellie said. "And I'm not sure they'd talk – we don't have any leverage like we did with Billy, and I don't think talking to detectives, even amateur ones, is really their thing."

"So, we've hit a dead end?" Clay said, "You know what would help?"

"I'm going to guess Italian coffee?" Ellie said, with a friendly scowl.

"You're not wrong," Clay beamed. "A strong cup of joe is the best thing to get the cogs turning again."

Ellie laughed. "Ok, well I certainly wouldn't say no to one. I think I've read one scrap of paper too many." She idly flicked over a small pile of notes and cards on the corner of the table, accidentally knocking a couple of them on the floor as she did. She bent over to pick them up again; a bank letter and a get-well card Eric must have been sent when he had the flu, by the look of the words scrawled in it. As she went to put the card back on the table, she could see the shadow of the edge of a thin sheet of paper fastened to one of the inside leaves by what looked like the sort of hinges her father had used for his stamp collections. She carefully peeled the paper away and turned it over to see it had been written on in scratchy blue-black ink.

"What you got there?" Clay said, leaning over the table to get a better look.

"A note of some sort," Ellie said, squinting to better read the small writing that looked like it had been written in a hurry. "Looks like Eric might have been trying to hide it."

"Good Lord," Georgie said, clapping her hand together sharply. "Do you mean we actually might have found something?"

"Possibly," Ellie said. "Let me just-" She started to scan the note, ready to read it out, then stopped; silently mouthing the words to herself.

> *"This is your only warning. Stay away from The Cat, stay away from the Blue Parakeet, and stay away from the band. If I catch you snooping around again there'll be trouble – big trouble. You can write whatever rubbish you want to about the show, but if I find out you plan on writing anything about what we both know I will make sure that it never gets to print, whatever that takes. I'm not a man to be messed with, you should know that. Keep your nose out and don't ask no more questions, or they might be the last ones you ever ask.*
> *Clay"*

"Are you alright, Ellie?" Georgie said, shifting in her chair towards her friend. "You've gone awfully pale."

Ellie stared at the paper for a moment before answering stutteringly. "Um… yes, yes I'm fine."

"Is it the note?" Clay said, standing to get a better view of it. Ellie quickly folded it and dropped it into her handbag.

"It's nothing," she said. "Just another shopping list."

"Ellie Blaine, you are a terrible fibber," Georgie said. "Tell me at once what that was, I simply forbid you from keeping any clues from us."

Ellie tried to laugh. "It… it was something, but I need… I can't tell you now. I'll tell you in a bit."

"Tell us over coffee," Clay said. "All this detecting has given me a righteous thirst."

Ellie drew a deep breath. "I'm sorry, Clay. I don't think I can. I'm feeling a little tired. I might have a lie down. Perhaps you should leave."

"That coffee's pretty strong," Clay said, smiling broadly. "It'll do you better than any shut eye."

"No," Ellie said firmly. "I really think you should leave now. I'm sorry. We… we can catch up later. Some other time."

Clay looked crestfallen for a moment, then quickly arranged his face back into a smile. "Sure thing, Ellie. You've been working hard, you need a rest. I'll just get my coat and see myself out."

Georgie stood sharply, throwing a disapproving glance at her friend then offering the way out to Clay. "I'm so sorry, Clay," she said. "I don't think Ellie is feeling herself. She's not normally this—"

"Tired?" Clay said, finishing Georgie's sentence with a softer word than she'd intended. "Sure – I get it. It was good to see you again, Ellie. I hope you feel better after some shut eye. Maybe I'll see you around again before we leave."

"What?" Ellie said, shaking herself out the deep thought she'd fallen into. "Oh, yes. Hopefully. Bye, Mr Clayton."

"Mr Clayton?" Clay shrugged deeply. "Sure, Miss Blaine. See you around."

Georgie saw Clay out of the door, with a final apology for her friend and a sympathetic pat on the arm, then turned to face Ellie, who had pulled the letter out to read again.

"Miss Eleanor Blaine. That was quite beastly of you, the poor chap. You could have let him down a little more gently. He's a fine fellow and he deserved—"

"Read this," Ellie said, placing the letter down on the table for Georgie to pick up. "And when you have, can you call Richard. Things have taken a turn, and we are going to need all the help we can get."

# CHAPTER 18

"ARE you alright, Ellie? Georgie made it sound rather urgent?" Richard had entered the room in such a hurry he hadn't even stopped to put his coat on the hanger and instead had flung it over the back of one of Georgie's armchairs, which made Ellie realise he really must be worried.

"I'm fine, Richard, thank you," Ellie said. "I think we may have had a breakthrough in the case, and not a welcome one I'm afraid."

"Ellie thinks Clay is the killer," Georgie said, picking up Richard's coat and putting it in its proper place.

"Clay?" Richard said, staring. "Surely not?"

"I found this," Ellie said. "Hidden among Eric's documents. It's a pretty clear threat, from Clay. He said he would act if Eric asked too many questions. It appears he was a man of his word."

Richard took the letter Ellie offered to him, carefully reading it while running his fingers through his thick, black hair. *"They might be the last ones you ever ask,"* he read out loud. "Well, he was certainly to the point. But I can hardly believe that of Clay, he doesn't seem the sort."

"Did Professor Berens seem the sort? Or Lucy? I'm not sure there is a 'sort', I've learned that much at least."

Richard put the letter down with a short, sharp expression of breath. "No, indeed. Well, I am quite taken aback. We should inform the police immediately of course."

"Of course," Ellie said. "I think I might take a step back from this one now. It feels a bit close to home. We should go to the station, give this to inspector Kinkaid."

"Absolutely," Richard said. "I would much prefer it if the police confronted Mr Parry rather than that you did. At least this once, I would appreciate it if you didn't put yourself in harm's way in your pursuit of justice. I think I've seen that enough times now."

"And so have I," Georgie said. "Just for a change, let's solve this one from the comfort of my sofa with a nice glass of G&T."

Ellie shook her head. "Yeah, I guess you are right. The important thing is that the killer is found, not that I get the credit."

Georgie raised her sculpted eyebrows. "Why don't you say that again, only this time at least try a teensy bit to make it sounds like you actually mean it."

Ellie laughed. "No, honestly. Rex can have this one. I liked Clay, it feels – wrong, to be the one who sees him…"

"Hanged," Georgie finished for her. "Yes, damned shame. Handsome chap, very talented. But then so was the prof, and I can't say I was sorry to see him hauled off in cuffs."

"Well, he did try to kill us," Ellie said. "And at least Clay hasn't done that. But it seems he might have killed three people, so it's not that easy to feel sorry for him."

"There is still a mystery you can solve though," Richard said.

"What's that?" Ellie said, taking Clay's note from Richard and putting it carefully down on the kitchen table.

"Even if we have perhaps discovered who killed those people, we still haven't got to the bottom of why the devil he would want to. What on earth was Mr Prendergast investigating that would turn a man to murder?"

"The only clue I've got on that is Eric's letter," Ellie said. "It isn't much to go on, and I suppose I should give that to the police as well, see if it makes more sense to them than it does to me."

"Do you have it to hand?" Richard said. "Maybe I could take a look. You never know, a fresh pair of eyes and so on."

"Be my guest," Ellie said. "There's not really very much on it that means anything to me. The handwriting is terrible, it took me a while to work out half of it, so I can tell you what I've read if it helps."

"That won't be necessary," Richard said. "I'm a doctor."

"She wants you to read the letter, not take its pulse," Georgie said, with a sideways glance.

"I'm a doctor, Georgie," Richard said stiffly. "And doctors have quite the most terrible handwriting you can imagine. Not mine, of course, but I do spend an inordinate amount of time reading the dreadful scrawl of any number of junior doctors; so I am sure I will be able to cope with whatever calligraphic abomination you put in front of me now."

"Here you go," Ellie said, handing him the letter. "We believe the town names are places the band was going to play. The list of names seems to be members of London street gangs, I've told you about those before. Oh, apart from the one he wrote just below the title of the list, I think it says "Lloyd" but it's basically just scribble."

Richard pulled up the letter to squint at, muttering to himself as he did, then turning it to show Ellie and jabbing his finger at the paper. "There's an 's' on the end. It's possessive."

"Possessive?"

"Yes, signalling the possession of some object by said Lloyd."

"I'm sorry?" Ellie said, following Richard's finger.

"Lloyd's. Apostrophe S. As in the bank."

"Really?" Ellie said. "Al was having some trouble with his bank, I think, from what I overheard. Perhaps it's related to that."

"If Clay was trying to ruin Al, that might fit," Georgie said. "Somehow. Though I'm not sure quite how."

"I just don't get why Clay would want to ruin his own show?" Ellie said, taking the letter back from Richard and carefully folding it.

"Maybe he didn't," Richard said. "Maybe he just wanted to hurt Brix. That fellow was rather an unpleasant chap, I can see how he might make enemies."

"And the reporter was killed for getting too close to Clay's plan?" Georgie said.

"And Jacques because he saw Clay poison Brix," Ellie said. "But then Clay was with us when Brix was poisoned. It makes no sense."

"Maybe Clay and The Cat are in cahoots," Georgie said, folding her arms sharply across her chest. "Ben too, perhaps. He certainly had good reason to dislike Brix."

"Well," Ellie said firmly. "All very confusing, but not our problem any more. I'm handing the evidence over to Rex and we'll see if he's as good as he says he is. If he can work this one out then he's right: he is a better detective than me."

"No one could be better than you, sweetie," Georgie said, giving Ellie a reassuring pat on the elbow. "You are the one who found Clay's note after he singularly missed it; anything Inspector Kinkaid comes up with will simply have been found by standing on your shoulders."

Ellie gave an unconvincing smile and put the letter in her bag, snapping it shut. "I suppose we should probably get to the station," she said. "Rex should still be there. I can just imagine his face when I give this over to him."

"I should imagine he will be most ungrateful," Georgie said, "and will then take all the credit for solving the case. But we shall know the truth, Ellie, and it is enough that your friends appreciate your efforts."

Ellie nodded a thank-you to Georgie, and offered her friends the way to the door ahead of her. "I should probably think about heading back to Melmersby after this," she said. "My London break wasn't quite what I expected it to be, and I'll be glad to get back to the quiet of home, I think."

"You must come down again," Georgie insisted. "Perhaps next time we can avoid the murder and mayhem that always seems to follow in your wake and just have a jolly good time."

"That would be good," Ellie said. "Or perhaps I should go and live in the middle of the woods somewhere, in a cave maybe? That might be the only way I can stop myself getting dragged into these things."

"I'm sure any cave you found would be chock-full of bodies, Ellie," Georgie said. "And the woods populated by murderous squirrels. Besides, you don't usually seem to take much dragging. I think you rather enjoy it, really."

Ellie gave a half-laugh. "I suppose I seem to have a gift for it, I just wish it didn't involve people I'd got attached to. A nice anonymous murder would make a change."

Richard frowned. "I'm not sure one should make light of such things," he said. "Gallows humour is all very well, but there are real gallows involved here."

Ellie held up her hand lightly in apology. "Sorry, Richard. You either laugh or you cry, and I've had my fair share of crying in the past. I just want to see justice being done, but it's hard sometimes."

Richard offered the same gesture of apology. "Of course, well, however it is done, we should see that it is. Shall we go?"

Georgie offered Richard his coat, which he took with a muttered thank you, and she opened the door, stepping aside slightly to let Ellie go through first.

"Thanks, Georgie," Ellie said, then stopped suddenly in her tracks. "Oh – wait, I left Clay's note on the table." She turned sharply to step back into the kitchen, quickly scanning the pile of more mundane paperwork to pick out the note, then stopped to read it through again one more time.

"It's not going to have changed since you last read it," Georgie called back through the alcove that led from the entrance hall to the kitchen. "You must have read it eight times at least by now."

"Sorry," Ellie called back. "Just a second, I—" Ellie stopped, staring at the note in her hand.

"Everything alright back there?" Georgie called again at the sudden silence of her friend.

"Oh yes," Ellie said, "I'm just thinking." She folded the note, slipping it back into her bag, then turned to pick up the bundle of envelopes from Melmersby that sat on the dresser, opening one to scan its contents quickly.

"She's thinking," Georgie confirmed to Richard, whose face was open in the manner of someone who was ready for anything to happen now. "Is that a good thing? I can never be sure."

Ellie stepped briskly back through the alcove with a broad smile on her face. "I've thought," she said with a wink at Georgie.

"Jolly good,' Richard said. "Let's get to the station then, before Inspector Kinkaid leaves."

"We're not going to the station," Ellie said brightly.

"We aren't?" Richard said, looking at Georgie for confirmation and getting only a shrug in return. "Where are we going then?"

"Well, first of all I'm going to use your telephone to call Livvy, if you don't mind, Georgie," Ellie said cheerfully. "Then I suggest we have a quiet evening and forget all about the murders until tomorrow, its going to be a long day, Georgie, so we should get an early night."

"Why?" Georgie said, eyeing her friend suspiciously. "What the blazes are you up to now?"

"How do you fancy a little girl's trip to the East End tomorrow evening, Georgie? Sorry Richard, you will have to stay behind for this one."

"What?" Georgie said, open-mouthed. "Why on earth–"

"Because Clay didn't write that note," Ellie said. "And he isn't the killer. But I'm starting to get the feeling we might be getting close to who is. And we'll get even closer, if you both don't mind doing what I say."

"When do we ever have the choice of that?" Georgie said. "Anything else, or is that it?"

"Just one more thing," Ellie said, grinning at her friend. "I wonder if I could borrow a necklace of yours? Something big and shiny and expensive looking would do the job just fine."

# CHAPTER 19

"NOW, I'm not saying this is the maddest idea you've ever had – and Lord knows it would be hard to choose one from the multitude – but… no, I will say it: this is the maddest idea you have ever had."

Ellie flashed a smile at her friend that managed to balance sympathy and slyness in equal measure. "I know what I'm doing, no-one will bother us. Don't you trust me yet? When have I ever gotten us into trouble before?"

"Oh, let me see. Shall I count the ways? No, I would need an abacus for that, and if I had one no doubt it would be about to be stolen off me in the next few minutes, along with my Great Aunt Mabel's diamond necklace that you are currently being a rather fetching shop window mannequin for, with half of the East End out looking for a bargain at the end of a knife blade!"

"I told you, you don't need to–"

"But seeing as you asked, there was that time you got us both driven into a swamp at gunpoint, shortly after we were nearly arrested for house-breaking. Oh, and that was after you got shot at and we were almost run over by hoodlums. Yes, and then there was that time we had a shotgun pointed at us by a highly emotional young man with a very shaky trigger finger, and the time…"

"It'll be different this time, trust me."

"You know I really only have myself to blame," Georgie said, glancing nervously over her shoulder at the narrow alleyways and darkened doorways of Brick Lane as they walked beneath a broken street lamp. "I could just say 'no'. 'No, Ellie Blaine, I am not going with you on a suicidal jaunt into a misty, bottomless bog in the middle of the night. No, I'm not going to walk the darkened streets of London gangland while you wear a big sign around your neck that says: 'please rob me'. I could just say 'no'. Next time I shall say 'no', just you wait and see."

"You're a good friend," Ellie said, putting her arm around Georgie's shoulder and pulling her in for a reassuring squeeze.

"Hmm," Georgie huffed. "Whether that remains mutual depends significantly on what happens in the next half hour."

Ellie gave a confident wave of her hand to dismiss Georgie's concerns, but she had to admit to herself that she had a few of her own. She was trusting the word of a thief, and hoping that what he had told her held good for everyone they might bump into in the next hour or so. And judging by the shifting shadows at the corner of the alley ahead, they were just about to find out whether she was right, or whether Georgie really did have a point after all.

"Evenin' ladies." A tall wiry man with a thin beard on his pock-marked face stepped out of the alley ahead of them. Behind them, two more now moved from the darkness of a shop entrance. "Lovely night for a stroll, ain't it. Only I think you might be lost."

"Oh, wonderful!" Georgie sighed out loud. "Well, here we go. That didn't take long." Georgie gave the man her hardest stare. "I suppose you are going to rob us? Well, this is entirely my friend's doing. Just for the record, I advised strongly against the whole ridiculous scheme. I shall give you a full account of the current worth of items about our person, that should help you get a good price from your 'fence' – I believe that's what you call them? But I should warn you we are both very well connected women and it shall bring a great deal of unwanted attention on you and your friends if either of us were to come to any harm."

The man grinned, showing a sparse row of broken and blackened teeth in his gummy mouth. "No one's gonna come to no harm, love. We just want to relieve you of a few bits and pieces. That necklace your friend's wearing looks mighty heavy for such a little lady, I wouldn't be a gentleman now, would I, if I didn't offer to take the load off her?"

Georgie glared at Ellie, saving some of the fire in her eyes for the men who had now moved up uncomfortably close behind them.

"Any pounds, shilling and pence, too, if you don't mind. Rings, watches, brooches. We're a bit like the rag an' bone man, us – we take any old stuff you might have." The man's companions laughed, the smaller of them coughing sharply as his chuckle caught up in his throat.

"Sticky weasel," Ellie said, holding the gaze of the tall man.

"I'm not sure it's the best idea to insult these gentlemen," Georgie said in a half-whisper, nodding her head towards the coughing man, who held a small blade in his hands. "Also, what sort of insult is—"

"What did you say?" the first man said, his thin jaw hung slackly open.

"Sticky weasel," Ellie said again, more firmly. "You heard me."

"Where did you hear that?" the man said, eyeing Ellie suspiciously.

"We did a favour for one of your friends," Ellie said, stepping away from the ever-closer attentions of the two men behind her. "And now I hope you'll be able to do one for us."

"Well," the man said, hands on his hips and elbows pointing out at a jagged angle. "Bless my soul, I didn't have you down for the type. Not the type at all. Still, a man's word is law here. It's your lucky night."

"'Ere, we're not just letting them go are we?" the coughing man said incredulously. "'Ave you seen what she's wearing round her neck? Nearly as big as a wren's egg, that sparkler. That'll keep us in clover for months."

The man standing beside him gave him a firm slap across the back of his head, and he winced sharply. The tall man stepped past Ellie and Georgie to get him to lift his head again. "Code of honour, Pat. Man's only as good as 'is word. It pains me too, but this is 'ow it is, or else what are we? Nuffin' more than common thieves. Remember that."

"Can someone explain what's going on?" Georgie said, her palms turned up as she looked around the circle of thieves and friends. "Are you robbing us or not? I'm a little confused."

"I'll explain later," Ellie said with a smile. "Now I wonder if you guys might like to earn an honest pound tonight? Well, semi-honest anyway."

The tall man looked at her distrustfully. "What you mean?"

"I've got thirty pounds in my bag," she said. "It's not a diamond necklace, I'm afraid, but it's not a bad night's takings."

"Not bad at all," the tall man said. "What you want for it?"

"Information," Ellie said.

"Now that is a pricey commodity in our line of work," the man said, whistling between his broken front teeth.

Ellie looked at Georgie imploringly. Her friend stared at her, confused for a moment, then shook her head briskly. "Oh no, no you don't. I am not giving these…gentlemen a single penny."

"What you got?" the man said, eyeing Georgie's clutch bag hungrily.

"You must have twenty pounds in there, right Georgie?" Ellie said. "Fifty enough for you?" she asked the man, who nodded. Georgie let out a sharp breath through her nose, scowling at Ellie for a second, before flipping open her bag and pulling out a large, crisp note that she handed to the man as if she were feeding a fish to a particularly snappy sea lion at London Zoo.

"Gratitudes, m'am," the man said, giving a slight bow that made Georgie curl her lip in response. "Now, what information is this buying?"

"I was just wondering what you could tell me about the Blue Parakeet. More specifically, who's been paying for you and your friends to go there."

The tall man shrugged. "Well, I think you may have just paid a lot for a very little, miss. Some geezer offered us tickets, no idea who he was; looked like he might be one of us, but not from this manor. He wasn't telling and we weren't asking. That's how a lot of things work round 'ere."

"But he wanted you to cause trouble at the show?"

"On the contrary, miss. He wanted us to behave ourselves like we was in Sunday church. Just some of us ain't very good at that." The tall man threw a hard glance at the coughing man, who shrugged sheepishly. "Can't say I'm one for jazz, miss. The old Music Hall is more my cup of tea, but we got a couple of free drinks so I can't complain, now can I?"

"Hmm," Ellie mused, fiddling self-consciously with the necklace that she was suddenly aware the coughing man had trouble keeping his eyes off. "I don't suppose you know a man called Lloyd?"

"Lloyd? Well the only one I know is old Lloyd George. He knew my father, and my father knew Lloyd George." The tall man let out a harsh, rasping laugh, and his companions joined in, sending the coughing man into an uncontrolled chesty hack; his friend having to slap him firmly on the back to return his breath. "Sorry miss," the tall man said, wiping the start of a tear from the corner of his eye, "old Music Hall joke."

Ellie looked, bemused, at Georgie who shook her head disdainfully. "So, you don't know anyone called Lloyd. None of your…friends?"

"No, miss," the man said, still fighting the urge to laugh at his own comment. "Never heard of him, if I'm honest."

"Thanks," Ellie said, "that's very helpful."

"Is it?" Georgie said. "I don't think we're getting very good value for our £50 so far. No offence."

"None taken, miss," the tall man said with a drop of his head.

"Just one final question," Ellie said, 'then we'll let you get on with your... business. Have any of your friends been to Birmingham recently? Or Manchester? Bradford maybe?"

The tall man shrugged. "We're not much for travel, miss. Like our home comforts, we do. Plus it don't do to tread on the toes of our... compatriots, in other towns. They're a particularly territorial lot, especially that Brummy crowd."

"Little Tom's been to Birmingham, he told me," the coughing man, who had finally cleared his throat, put in.

"Little Tom?" Ellie said.

"Aye. His name's Tom Little, see, so we all calls 'im Little Tom, even though he is actually quite a normal sized fella."

"How frightfully original," Georgie said. "It must have taken an age to come up with that one."

Ellie gave her a look that suggested she might want to listen more than speak just now, especially with the price of words on this particular street. "Could I talk to him, maybe?"

The tall man shook his head. "Not a chance, I'm afraid. He's taking a little holiday, at His Majesty's pleasure, right now. Dartmoor, I think."

Ellie nodded. "But he was in Birmingham?"

"Aye, miss," the coughing man said. "Took a trip there a couple of months back, bought his missus a nice little gold chain too when he come back, he showed me it. Well, I think he bought it. He had a bit of an eye for a trinket, you see. Which is kind of how he ended up in Dartmoor, but–"

"That's enough, Pat," the tall man said. "The lads here do a lot of business for a lot of people, but we don't tend to talk about it. Which is how our clients like it. Now, you've said the code words and you've paid us well, but I think we've probably come to the end of your tariff, if you don't mind."

Ellie nodded. "Thanks, you've been a real help."

The man returned the nod. "Now, we are gentlemen of honour, but not everyone around here is quite so strict in following the rules, so I suggest you put that pretty bauble of yours out of sight, and get yourselves back to the right side of town as quick as you like. 'Ere, allow me." The man put his fingers to his mouth and let out a sharp, piercing whistle. At the sound, a grey car that had been passing on the other side of the road made a sudden turn, pulling up alongside them. The window was prized open and the bald head of a slightly chubby, middle-aged man appeared out of it.

"Alright Arfur? Where to?"

"Not for me," the tall man said. "These two ladies are heading back into town. Make sure you take them direct, now, not all round the mulberry bush like you take most people."

"I don't know what you mean, Arfur," the man said, less than convincingly. "I only ever go the quickest way. Hop in, ladies."

Ellie opened the door for Georgie, who eased herself into the slightly worn back seat as Ellie got in beside her. "Could you take us to Costermongers Row, please," Ellie said. "Number 24."

"Costermongers Row?" the taxi driver said, frowning. "You sure about that?"

"Yes," Georgie said, mirroring the cabbie's expression, "are you sure about that?"

"Is it far?" Ellie said.

"Well, no," the cab driver said, "just round the corner, but there ain't nuffin' there."

"How do you mean?"

The driver held his hands. "All shut up, ain't it. Rising damp, rotten as a month-old egg sandwich, them houses. Whole street's condemned, ain't no-one livin' there no-more."

"Oh," Ellie said, the ghost of a smile playing on her lips. "My mistake then. Could you just take us to Grosvenor Square?"

"Grosvenor Square? Very posh," the cab driver said, putting his free arm on his seat-back to turn his head towards the rear seat. "What's a pair of ladies like you doing out in this part of town at this time?"

Georgie leaned forward, her fingers together as if she was about to deliver a sermon. "We have just paid those gentlemen an extortionate amount of money so that they would talk to us, and now we are paying you an extortionate cab fare specifically so that you do not talk to us. It has been a trying night."

The man coloured slightly and turned his attention back to the road. Ellie gave her friend an amused look.

"I don't know what you're looking so pleased with yourself about, either," Georgie said sharply. "How difficult would it have been for you to tell me exactly what you planned to do? I've gone along with your schemes in blissful ignorance before, but now I think you do it deliberately, just to wind me up. I am not some clockwork toy for your amusement!"

Ellie winced slightly, offering her hand to her friend, who refused it for a moment before taking it with just enough of an expression of disdain on her face. "I'm sorry, Georgie. I didn't want to do it on my own and I always feel a little safer with you there. I should have told you the whole plan, you're right. I will next time, I promise."

"Next time?" Georgie said, pulling in her neck. "I'm rather hoping that that might be it for the whole 'let's put ourselves in mortal danger' thing. At least for a while."

"At least for a while," Ellie said, and she squeezed her friend's hand with a grin.

# CHAPTER 20

"WELL I sure appreciate the invite, Ellie. I was starting to think I must have said something wrong last time." Ellie half-stood as Clay pulled out the seat beside her at the table of the Cafe Royale, and he dropped into the chair with an easy slouch. "Good to see you all as well."

By the way he said the last part, Ellie wasn't entirely convinced of how pleased Clay was that their dinner date had turned out to be a party of seven, but she was glad to see him nonetheless. Not least because it gave her a chance to apologize for the rude way she'd dismissed him the last time they met.

"I'm sorry about that, Clay," she said. "I was just very tired, and feeling frustrated at going through all those documents without getting anything useful from them."

"I thought you found something in them?" Clay said, pulling his chair in closer to the table and signalling to the waiter that he was ready for a coffee.

"Oh, I thought I did," Ellie said, "but it turned out to be something different."

Georgie looked up at the ceiling, subtly shaking her head to herself. Around the table, Sarah – who had walked into the sumptuous dining room so firmly attached to Richard's arm that Ellie wondered if they might need a bench seat for dinner – was in a deep discussion with her companion on the merits of sour cream vs cream cheese to accompany caviar and blinis. Liz, who was sitting next to Louis, had tried on at least three occasions to engage him in conversation, but had now decided it would be more productive to give all her attention to the label on the bottle of Krug champagne in front of her, and had re-read it several times now. Louis – who Ellie had persuaded to join them with the promise of as many glasses of his favourite Cognac as he wanted – was sitting right across the table from Ellie, but it seemed to her his mind was very much in a different place.

"So, how has the detective work been going since I last saw you?" Clay said, leaning aside with a nod of thanks to allow the immaculately dressed waiter to place a silver coffee pot beside him. "You caught him yet?"

"Not yet," Ellie said. "But I've been working on it."

"Yes, what have you been doing with yourself, Ellie?" Georgie said, delicately wiping a crumb of crustless cucumber sandwich from the side of her mouth with a lace serviette then turning to Clay. "As usual, she's not said a thing about it to her best friend. She's been up at the crack of dawn and back after bedtime, I've hardly seen her the last couple of days."

"I took Richard's advice, on the importance of a good education," Ellie said. "I've been to school – studying music and French."

"I've given her a couple of lessons; a natural with the accent, let me say," Liz said brightly, eager to engage with something other than a bottle.

"French, not music, I assume," Georgie said. "You have many talents, Liz darling, but from what I remember of choral practice at school you hold a tune like a sieve holds water."

Liz laughed, and Ellie shook her head. "No, Liz is an excellent French teacher, but the music I learned was at a little place close to the Blue Parakeet – Chappell & Co – the store manager there was very helpful."

"So, what's your plan with all your new-found learning, then?" Georgie said. "Are you intending to run off to Paris to join the burgeoning jazz scene there?"

Ellie took a sip of her tea, puckering her mouth at the cold stew it had made while she'd been distracted. "No, I was just learning a bit more about saxophones. I even had a go on one, they're pretty difficult to play. I couldn't even make a proper sound, it makes me appreciate your talent even more, Louis."

Louis looked up at his name, as if he had suddenly re-entered the room and was now entirely, body and mind, at the table, for a moment at least. He said nothing, but raised his hand in acknowledgement of the praise then took another sip from his bulbous brandy glass.

"What are you up to, Ellie?" Georgie said, narrowing her eyes suspiciously. "And why am I getting the feeling you are about to cause mayhem again?"

"Oh, that reminds me," Richard said, suddenly snapping his fingers and taking the opportunity to lean out of the zone of Sarah's close attention. "Talking of mayhem, I'm afraid you have sent poor Mrs Madison into a maelstrom of emotions. I keep trying to tell her that I am no longer her employer, but that doesn't seem to stop her telegrams. Nor, come to think of it, does it stop her charging those telegrams to my account. I must talk to her about that."

"Ah," Ellie said. "Yes, I think I may have left her a little in the lurch, although with no one in the house at the moment I thought she could spare Livvy for a couple of days."

"Livvy?" Georgie said, leaning across the table to pick up the last of the sandwich portions, having decided she'd waited just long enough for anyone else to take the opportunity that it wouldn't be impolite. "What have you roped her into?"

"You can ask her yourself," Ellie said, "she'll be here tomorrow."

"Livvy's coming to London?" Georgie said, not waiting this time to finish her sandwich before speaking. "Now I know you are up to something."

"I just thought she might enjoy the chance to see London, visit the jazz club – she likes her music. Maybe we could all meet up again, tomorrow, at the Blue Parakeet?"

"There's not much going on there at the moment," Clay said. "It's all closed up apart from our rooms. I can check with Al if he'll open it up for us."

"Thank you, Clay," Ellie said. "It would be good if Al was there too. And Tommy and Spats as well, if you don't mind asking them. Oh, and perhaps we could send an invite to Rex Kinkaid?"

"Eleanor Blaine!" Georgie said, putting her hands down firmly on the table. "I knew it!"

Ellie winked at her friend. "You'll be there too, Louis?" she said, leaning across the table to catch the Cat's attention.

Louis looked up, expressionless. "Sure, I'm staying there and I ain't got nowhere better to go."

"Thank you," Ellie said. "Well, I have to rush I'm afraid, I need to make some arrangements for Livvy's stay, I'll catch you all tomorrow." Ellie stood to mumbled protests from some of the table, and nodded to the waiter to bring her coat.

"Yeah, see you tomorrow," Clay said with a look of friendly resignation.

"I'm really sorry to rush off so soon," Ellie said. "When do you head back to the States? Perhaps we could catch up, go to lunch, before you leave?"

"Saturday," Clay said. "I got a couple more days."

"Great," Ellie said. "Well, I think I only need one more, so lets do something Friday maybe?"

Clay smiled. "I'd sure like that," he said.

Ellie returned the smile then turned to allow the waiter to help her on with her coat. She stepped towards the door, then suddenly turned back. "Oh, I've left my bag on the table," she said. "Louis, could you just reach across and grab it for me?"

Louis looked blankly at Ellie and shrugged, leaning over to take the small clutch bag where Ellie had placed it next to her empty plate and turning in his chair to hand it to her.

Ellie pulled the bag up onto her shoulder then leaned in to give him a gentle peck on his cheek in thanks. "Merci beaucoup d'avoir aidé, Monsieur Chat."

"Pas de problème, Mademois–," Louis started. The Cat dropped his hands suddenly to his side, glancing around the table to where Clay sat open-mouthed and Georgie had just spluttered out a mouthful of tea that was now melting the small tray of macarons the waiter had just delivered. He stood in an instant, hauling back his chair angrily, half tipping it over, and turned, without looking back or waiting for his coat, to march out of the door, almost knocking a tray of cream buns from a startled waiter's hands as he went.

Ellie turned back to the stunned table and shrugged. "Right, see you all tomorrow then!"

# CHAPTER 21

"NOW ain't this something," Rex Kinkaid said, a not-so-subtle sneer playing on his thin lips. "You've got the whole cast here, I see. And a few faces I don't know. Well, you've picked the right spot for putting on a show. That's what this is, right? A show?"

Ellie shook her head. "I don't know what you mean."

"Oh come off it," Rex said, throwing his arms out wide and looking in turn at each of the two armed police officers who flanked him. "You've got us all here because you think you've found out who the killer is, and you want to make a song and dance about it, show everyone what a great detective you are. Well, I cannot wait to hear the details of your brilliant deduction, Miss Blaine. Ain't that right boys? The little lady is going to show us how it's done."

The two officers laughed in unison; practiced laughs that Ellie imagined were requirements of their jobs when working with Inspector Kinkaid.

"Do you know who the killer is?" Richard said.

"I have an idea," Ellie said. "But we'll come to that in a minute."

"I'm guessing it's someone here?" Tommy Marvin said, nervously glancing around the group that was assembled on the half-lit and chilly, empty dance floor of the Blue Parakeet; some standing, others on chairs they'd pulled down from the tables, and Clay, Cat and Ben sitting on the edge of the stage.

"Well it ain't me," Livvy said, chirpily. "I only just got here, and I ain't really got a clue what is going on. I thought we were going to see some jazz?"

"Sorry love," Rex said, "no jazz today, I've got a feeling this is going to be more like a pantomime."

"Oh no it isn't!" Georgie called out theatrically. Rex muttered something incomprehensible under his breath.

"What have you found out?" Al said, shifting his heavy frame uneasily in his chair. "Did you learn anything more about Eric?"

"A little," Ellie said. "Enough."

"So come on then," Rex growled. "Put us out of our misery. Who did it?"

Ellie slowly picked up a glass of water, bringing it up to hold just short of her lips before speaking. "It was Clay."

"What?" Clay blurted out, staring in bemusement at Ellie as gasps broke out around the room. Ellie took a long draw of the water.

"And I presume you have evidence for this?" Rex said, looking again at his two officers. "Tell us how you came to this brilliant discovery. I guess you can produce something for us now?"

"Sorry," Ellie said, gulping. "Dry throat, needed a drink to clear it for a second there. I was just saying, it was Clay who helped me see it, so thanks Clay."

Clay shook his head slowly, eyes wide open. "Don't do that to me Ellie!"

Ellie smiled subtly. "As did Livvy, and of course Georgie, Liz, Richard. It's been a team effort. And now I can be pretty sure that the person who killed Eric was the same person who killed Brix and Jacques, and that they killed them all for the same reason – even if they didn't always intend to."

"Gosh, you sound like a real detective," Georgie said, quickly correcting herself with a glance at Rex. "Because that is what you are, naturally."

"Thanks Georgie," Ellie said. "I think!"

"What was the motive?" Spats asked. "Money? It's usually money."

"Eric was killed because he was on the verge of a scoop – something he believed would make his name as a journalist and shake up the world of jazz. But some things are kept secret for a reason, and someone was determined that he wouldn't be able to reveal this one. He was—"

"I didn't kill nobody!" Cat leapt down from the stage, standing with his arms crossed tight across his narrow chest, his eyes burning with anger, or fear, Ellie wasn't sure which. "Yeah, that reporter guy was on to me, but I didn't kill him. I ain't never hurt no one. You got the wrong man."

"Is that so, Louis?" Ellie said. "Or do you prefer to go by Cat these days? Or is it Thierry? Amos? It must be difficult to keep track."

Cat snarled. "You're a smart lady, Miss Blaine. Yeah, you got me there, but you ain't so smart if you think I killed that Eric fella, or Brix, or anyone."

Ellie nodded. "Why would I think you killed anyone, Louis?"

"Amos," Louis said. "You might as well call me Amos. Amos Jackson. That's my name. My real name."

"You were the guy on that record? The Sweet Six?" Clay said, staring at his friend as if it were the first time he'd seen him. "That can't have been you. It didn't sound nothing like you."

"Yeah, you're right about that," Cat said. "Didn't sound nothing like me, or you could say I don't sound nothing like him. Brix never worked that one out."

"I mean, am I the only one here who has no clue what is happening now?" Georgie said. "Why were you pretending to be someone you aren't? And what does that have to do with murder?"

"Brix," Cat snarled. "I wanted to make that man pay. I didn't kill him, but there sure were times when I wanted to. But I wanted something more for him, something that would hurt him more. I didn't want to kill him, I wanted to kill his reputation, and whoever done him in took that chance away from me."

"What happened, Amos?" Ellie said.

"It was a long time ago," Cat said, leaning back with a sigh against the stage. "Right about the time I cut that record with The Sweet Six. Brix was just building up his reputation as the music man on the scene, the big time band leader everyone wanted to work with. Well, I saw he was holding auditions for his band, in that big new theatre at Midway Gardens. So, I took myself along to see if I could cut it in the big time.

"I was sure nervous; all the top cats in town were there, all the players, the folks I looked up to and admired. I was shakin' like a leaf, but I knew I was good, I knew I could stand with 'em. Brix had 'em all sat there, all the best musicians in Chicago, watching as we went up in turn. Come to my spot, and I walked up them steps to the stage, knowing this was my chance, my time."

Ellie could see that Amos, cool as he was, now had tears swelling in his eyes, as he shook his head. "Say, could someone fix me a drink? You got any of that Napoleon Brandy in here?"

Richard glanced at Al, who stared blankly for a moment then nodded towards the bar. Richard stepped up to lean over the counter and take down a large green bottle. He handed the bottle to Cat, who pulled the stopper then took a long draw straight from the top.

"So, I pull my sax up, and I start to blow," he continued. "I was plannin' to play a little blues piece I did with the Sweet Six, but I didn't get but two bars in and Brix, he puts up his hand and calls me out to stop. So I says: 'is that all you want, Mr Riley, sir?', and he says: 'that's all I need'."

"So I ask him: 'what do you mean, sir?' And he just says: 'what's your name, boy?' So I tell him, I say: 'my name's Amos Jackson, sir.' And he says: 'well, Amos Jackson, there's a few of the guys who aren't sitting here to listen to you, so I'm gonna call them back in. I want everyone to hear you'. And he calls them back in to take a seat; I see people there I know, friends, guys I respect, even cats from my own band. And then he asks me to play the same thing again. So I do, and he stops me right at the same point."

Ellie could see Amos's hands clenching and unclenching, the tears in his eyes now replaced by a cold fire, his expression so filled with hate that anyone might think he could have killed Brix without missing a heartbeat. He paused for a moment, to draw a deep breath, then spoke again.

"He stands up, looking round at all the guys in their seats, and he calls out. He says: 'Now, if any of you guys wanted to know what I'm looking for, what my music is all about, just take a look at Amos Jackson here. Take a look, and then do exactly the opposite to what he just did up there on that stage'.

"Well, I couldn't talk, but to say 'why?' And he turns to me and he says: 'Every man who ever picked up an instrument has a voice. You can't change it, you can't hide it, you can't fake it. And I hear your voice, Amos Jackson, and I mightn't remember your face, I certainly won't remember your name, but I will never forget your voice. I will never forget just how down-home, hick-square, low-rent vaudeville, terrible it is. Get off my stage and stop wasting my time, these gentlemen's time, and your own time. If you want to earn an honest dollar, go and get a job shining shoes, 'cos that's all you'll ever be good for'."

Georgie shook her head. "What an absolutely beastly man. I know one shouldn't speak ill of the dead, but really!"

"You ok, Amos?" Clay said, leaning in to check on his friend, who now took another long gulp from the brandy bottle.

"I'm just fine," Amos said. "Just fine."

"So what happened?" Ellie said. "After that? What did you do?"

"Well, for a while I took his advice," Amos said. "He broke me, just as sure as I was a dry twig. I sold my saxophone and I took a job tending bar in a club for a while, only I couldn't stand to hear the music they played each night, couldn't deal with the memories, so I quit and started shining shoes down at LaSalle Street Station. Thought I'd never play again. But then the war come in Europe, and after a while they started looking for boys from here to go over there and help out. Well, I thought I ain't got nothing else to do with my life, so I signed up and they shipped me over to France.

"After all the fightin' stopped, I figured I had nothing to go back for, so I stayed in Paris, took a job as a busboy in a fancy hotel there. Then one night, some cat comes in, American guy, guy like me. And he hears my accent, so we get to talking, and it turns out he's a sax player. He tells me that a few cats like him stayed in Paris after the war, and that they are cooking up a little jazz scene in the city. Asks if I want to see a show. Well, I figured it had been long enough that I could bear to listen to jazz again, so I goes with him to a little dive bar in Montmartre. I get there and the guys are blowing hot, real swinging. At first I gets to shakin', all them memories coming back. But then I hear something, something like the voice of an angel singing in that saxophone. And I know that I have to get back to it, that that is who I am, that I was born with the music in me.

"So I buys an old sax from one of those cats, a little beat-up diamond I called Jessica, and I start to play all over again. Only this time I have a fire burnin' in me. I have a mission. I have a vision – of me, standing on that stage in Chicago, and blowing hot, while Brix begs me to join his band. And I tell you, I tell you now, that mission drives me like a steam train. I practice, night and day, hardly sleepin', hardly eatin' – I just practice, and I study, and I learn from all the cats in Paris, from all the records that are shipped in from New York, from anywhere I can. I work and I work and I work, to change my voice, to be who I was meant to be, to show that fool Brix he was wrong.

"Two years I work like a dog to be the Cat. Gave myself the name Thierry Renault, 'cos I didn't want no trace of where I'd been, or where I was going, not if I was gonna catch old Brix out. Then, one day, back in 1920, I'm standing at the Left Bank, looking down into that river there in Paris. I busked there, to earn a crust when I weren't sitting in an all-nighter at the club. I looked down at my reflection in the water, and I didn't see Amos no more, I didn't see Thierry. I saw Louis, I saw the Cat. I picked up my saxophone and I started to blow, and the whole of Paris just stopped, stopped to listen to me. I saw men stop on the street and take off their hats, I saw women cry, I saw cars pull into the side of the road; all from hearing the Cat blow. And I knew then, it was time for the Cat to go home."

"Well, I should imagine not sleeping for two years would make a man go a bit doolally," Georgie whispered to Ellie, "but in his case, it seems to have made him in-Seine!"

Ellie glared at her friend, shaking her head incredulously.

"In-Seine? Like the river? Get it? No? Oh, suit yourself!"

"So what was your plan when you got back? You got the gig with Brix, wasn't that enough?" Ellie said, ignoring Georgie.

Amos shook his head. "When we get back from this tour, we would have been booked in to play the Midway Gardens for the first time as the Blue Notes. All the old cats would be there, the guys who watched Brix humiliate me. And I was set to take that stage, and I had it all planned out – I would play them same old bars from the same old blues song; just them two little bars that Brix allowed me back then. Then I would walk off that stage, and I would leave Brix there – in front of everyone – exposed as the fraud he is. His magic ears are made of cloth, and every cat in Chicago would know it, and I would hang him out to dry just like he did to me all them years ago."

"But of course, now you can't, because he's dead," Ellie said.

"Yep," Cat said. "And I never thought I'd say this, but I sure am sorry that he died, 'cos whoever did it, they didn't just take Brix's life, they took my revenge from me."

"Revenge is a two-edged sword," Richard said softly. "I'm glad you proved him wrong, but trust me, your victory was in becoming who you were meant to be, it would have done you no good to hurt him, it wouldn't take away the pain of what he did to you."

Amos drank from the bottle again, silently studying Richard for a moment before speaking. "I figure you are right," he said. "I wanted to close a wound I never thought would heal. But, seeing him drop dead like that, right in front of me – I never, not in a hundred lifetimes, thought I would feel sorry for Brix. But I do, and as soon as I got that feeling, I felt the hurt leave me. For the first time in nearly ten years, I don't hate him no more."

"And you didn't kill him, or anyone else," Ellie said. "Thank you for telling us that, it must have been hard for you."

Amos said nothing, but raised the bottle and took another sip.

"So, if Cat – sorry, Amos – didn't kill Eric to stop him exposing his past, just who exactly did?" Richard said.

"Well you see," Ellie said, "Eric wasn't just working on one story; while he was investigating Amos he stumbled on another scoop. He didn't have the whole picture, not enough to publish, but enough to use the story for another purpose."

"Another one?" Georgie said. "Are you going to tell me Clay's name is really Bob and that he played the triangle in a German oompah band?"

Ellie almost laughed. "No, nothing like that. Eric found out something else about the tour. His mistake was to try to use that as leverage to get Cat to talk to him; he thought Cat's was the bigger story, but it was the other one that someone thought it was worth killing him for. Livvy, could you tell everyone where you've been the last couple of days."

Livvy shook herself, surprised to have been called up and seemingly as confused as everyone else. "Me?" she said, pointing to herself. "Well, I've been bloomin' everywhere – Birmingham, Bradford, all over the shop."

"Why?" Georgie said, looking at Ellie suspiciously.

"Well, 'cos Miss Ellie asked me to, that's why, and I works for Miss Ellie."

"What kind of work, this time?" Richard said.

"She asked me to go and visit some theatres," Livvy said. "See if I couldn't use my Yorkshire charms to sweet talk some information out of the gentlemen what works there, that's what she said. Well, my Alfie didn't like that, but I 'as to do as I am asked by them what pays my wages."

"Sorry," Ellie said. "I hope I didn't ask you to do anything that made you uncomfortable."

"Livvy waved her hand. "Nah! I didn't mind. Took my Alfie with me, just made him sit outside while I did my sweet talking," she said. "Quite exciting really, being an investigator and all, even if I'm not really sure what I was investigating."

"What did you investigate?" Clay said, scratching at the back of his head.

"Tickets," Livvy said. "I was finding out about tickets."

"Do you want to tell everyone what you found out?" Ellie said.

"Yeah, well it was a bit of an odd thing," she said. "All them theatres was putting on Brix Riley's show, and they had all sold loads and loads of tickets. Hundreds, or thousands even. But turns out they'd nearly all been bought by the same person. The lad in Birmingham – he was awful shy, but I got it out of him by buying him an ice-cream, proper nice it were, with sprinkles and everything – he said all the tickets was bought by some scruffy bloke who sounded like was from London, all in used notes, all crumply and everything. And the funny thing was, like I told you on the phone the other day Miss Ellie, he made sure to give him an address to send the money back to, if there was refunds or anything."

"And that address, it turns out, is of a condemned and empty house in Costermongers Row," Ellie said. "An anonymous address, for someone who wanted to hide where the money came from, and where it was going. No doubt some arrangement had been made for the money to be picked up."

"But what on earth for?" Richard said.

"Because the person who wanted to stop the show, the person who got street thieves to populate the Blue Parakeet these last few nights, wanted to be sure they wouldn't be out of pocket when the show ended. In fact they wanted to be very much better off if it was."

"And that person is…?" Georgie prompted.

Ellie looked around the huddled group in turn, then turned her gaze on the flushed figure nervously wringing his hands in the chair beside her. "That person is Al Maguire."

Al stood up so fast his chair toppled backwards with a clatter to the floor. His fleshy forehead was glistening with sweat and he pulled sharply at his tightening collar. "That is ridiculous!" he shouted, looking around the shocked faces in the room. "Absolutely ridiculous, I'm losing a fortune with the show being stopped."

"Yes," Ellie said, "a considerable fortune. A far bigger fortune than you would have made if you'd been relying on genuine ticket sales. It seems Tommy and Spat's observation that there wasn't much of an audience for jazz in England was right. That's why you had to fake the ticket sales."

Al laughed, a cold laugh. "What, so I spend my money on tickets and then just get it back? What sort of a motive is that?"

"It was the names, you see," Ellie said. "Who are the names?, that's what Eric's letter said. Not 'what are the names?' And then Richard spotted it – it was Lloyd's, not Lloyd. It wasn't a person, or the bank; it was the insurance agency. I thought the other long number looked familiar, but I didn't spot it until Livvy sent over the documents I had to sign for Melmersby Hall – four letters, six digits. A policy number for Lloyds of London."

"Of course!" Richard said, snapping his fingers. "The Names!"

"Names?" Clay said, looking questioningly between Ellie and Richard.

"Names is what they call the great and the good – well the loaded and the speculative – who put up money for insurance schemes at Lloyd's of London," Georgie said. "It's more like a gambling syndicate than an insurance broker, if you ask me. You can insure pretty much anything, and the Names will take on the risk – if it goes well they make a packet, and if it goes badly they take the hit."

"Exactly," Ellie said. "They'll take on anything, as long as they believe the venture is profitable enough to be worth the risk. And Al, after taking out a loan against the club, had enough money to put up a very big insurance premium as well as buy his own tickets."

"Why buy his own tickets?" Richard said, glancing at Al, who had now sat down and seemed to be having trouble breathing.

"I imagine he was insured against his losses. Is that right, Al? They weren't going to pay out if you simply cancelled a show with no ticket sales."

Al shook his head, looking even more nervous than he had before.

"They would have agreed to pay out to the value of whatever Al stood to make from the tour. If he was going to claim the amount he wanted, he needed to prove he would have made a fortune. He just needed to show ticket numbers, then back it up with a full house for the Blue Parakeet, so it seemed the show was wildly successful, when in reality he had probably sold less than half the seats for any night here, and almost none outside of London. Al had mortgaged his house to pay for the tour, and when he realised it was going to be a financial failure, he turned to insurance fraud in desperation. Eric found out about this, and tried to blackmail him into making Cat talk to him. I'm sure Al never intended to kill him, it wasn't premeditated. You just lost your cool for a minute, didn't you, Al? You saw red, saw your whole future disappearing before your eyes, and lost control."

"This is preposterous," Al blurted, 'no-one believes this, do they?"

The two officers, at a nod from Rex, moved in beside his chair. It seemed they did.

"What about Brix? Jacques?" Georgie said.

"After Al failed to stop the show by breaking Amos's sax—"

Amos suddenly lunged across the room, grabbing for Al, who half-fell back in his seat. Clay moved swiftly to hold his friend back, talking softly into his ear as he pulled him away.

Ellie nodded to Clay. "After that failed, he got even more desperate. The longer the tour went on without shows being cancelled, the more money Al would lose. He was shaken by Brix's death, because he never originally planned it, he never wanted it. He thought the sax would be enough. But by then he had no choice, he had sunk too much money into his plan to back out."

"But Al was here," Georgie said. "He was in the room when Brix was poisoned."

"Yes," Ellie said. "Because this is the room Brix was poisoned in. I worked that out, with a little help from Clay and the guys at the music shop. Clay told me that Tommy used to play clarinet and that the two instruments were quite similar. And that's why Jacques died."

"Jacques? How?" Richard said.

"Brix wasn't poisoned in the dressing room, he was poisoned on stage. By cyanide that someone had coated a clarinet reed with, the reed he slipped into Brix's instrument when he went on stage to close the curtains for the interval. I imagine your friends on the street were useful for sourcing the cyanide, Al?"

Al was shaking his head so violently that droplets of sweat were spraying around him, leaving spots of dark stain on the parquet wood dance floor.

"And how did that kill Jacques?" Spats said, staring unbelievingly at his old business rival.

"Al retrieved the poison reed when he went to close the curtain again after Brix fell. He then ran to the back door, where he threw it out into the alley before smoking his cigarette. Jacques must have found it, thinking it was his lucky day. You see, it turns out that you can use the same type of reed from a clarinet in a saxophone. Jacques found it and put it in his, twhich is why his saxophone sounded so much clearer that night when we saw him after leaving the club. He had a new reed – a deadly new reed."

"You can't prove any of this!" Al barked. "It will never stand up in court."

"We have the insurance number, for a policy that will be in your name," Ellie said. "And we have the names of the people you employed to carry out your dirty work with the tickets – one of them at least. He's currently in Dartmoor prison, where I am sure he will be only too happy to tell the police everything, in exchange for a shorter sentence. And the police have Jacques' saxophone. I called them just before we started here; they'll be running tests on the reed right about now, I should think."

"Ok," Rex Kinkaid growled. "Cuff him boys."

The two officers hauled Al, still protesting, from his seat, one struggling to stop his wriggling while the other fumbled with the cuffs.

"What about Clay's letter?" Richard said. "Presumably Al sent that to throw the police off the scent?"

Clay looked confused and Ellie raised a finger to assure him she would explain it all in a minute.

"No, Al didn't send that. No one sent it. It was put in the card for me to find."

Rex glanced nervously at Ellie, his upper lip momentarily twitching.

"I knew it wasn't sent by Clay," Ellie said, "or any of the band. Because whoever sent it was English, not American."

"Well, I'm impressed, but I don't see how–" Richard started.

"Rubbish," Ellie said sharply.

"I beg your pardon!" Richard said, a hint of rose colouring his high cheekbones.

"Rubbish," Ellie repeated, "'*Whatever rubbish you want to write*' – that's what the letter said. I've been in England so long I didn't pick up on it at first. No American would say 'rubbish' – trash? Yes, or garbage. Never rubbish."

"So why don't you think it was Al?" Georgie said.

"Because Al has worked enough with Americans to know that, and besides, Al didn't know Eric was about to expose him. If he was trying to cover his tracks he would have had to have sent it after he killed Eric, so it would never have been hidden. It would have to have been done by someone who had access to Eric's documents after he died, and who really, really wanted to see me make a fool of myself by accusing the wrong person."

Rex Kinkaid now stepped towards Ellie, his face a dark red and fists clenched. "What are you implying? Are you saying I planted evidence? Are you aware how serious an accusation that is? I hope you have got proof of that, young lady, because if you haven't you are going to be in a whole lot of trouble if you try to tell people that's what I did."

Ellie shook her head. "Unfortunately, I can't prove it. But it's a bit of a coincidence, don't you think? And like you said, there are no such things as coincidences."

"Yeah," Rex snarled. "But you can't prove it."

"She doesn't need to prove it," Georgie said. "Because she's already proved something beyond all reasonable doubt."

"Oh yeah? And what's that then, love?" Rex sneered.

"She's proved she is a far, far better detective than you will ever be!"

The larger of the two officers, who was still wrestling Al, burst into laughter as Rex turned an even darker scarlet than he had before. The laughing policeman's grip loosened on Al, who took the moment to turn away from his hold and grab at the pistol at the officer's hip, drawing it in one movement and grabbing Ellie around the neck in another. He pushed the gun barrel into Ellie's temple, holding her in a firm armlock, and started moving slowly back towards the door.

"Nobody follow me, you understand? Nobody! I will shoot her, I swear."

Ellie tried to keep her head still, not to force any panicked reaction from Al as he dragged her back with him, closer towards the exit.

"Don't be stupid, Mr Maguire," Rex said, holding up his hands to signal a need for calm. "You won't get far, you won't get away. Where do you think you're going to go?"

"No?" Al said, pausing to catch a heavy breath. "No, you're right, but I am done, I am finished. And she did this to me. If I'm done for then so is she."

He raised his hand to push the barrel hard into the side of Ellie's head, and she closed her eyes, waiting for the moment, hoping it would be over before she felt it.

And then she felt the weight of a heavy body, fast and decisive, crashing into her and Al, knocking her to the floor as it hit, sending Al falling the other way. She turned her head to see Al, struggling violently, as Richard gripped his gun arm, twisting to try to prize the weapon from his hand. Al's arm turned at an unnatural angle, burying itself between the two men as he let out a sharp cry of pain, then a gunshot, and silence.

Neither man moved for a moment, as Ellie turned on her side on the floow to reach Richard. He sat up slowly, his hand holding his chest, his white shirt now stained across its full breadth in deep crimson.

"Richard!" Ellie called out. "You're hurt. Are you alright? Someone call an ambulance!"

She looked desperately around the room as Clay ran towards the foyer and the club telephone.

"I'm afraid it's too late for that," Richard said somberly.

"It can't be," Ellie said, her eyes filling with the deep swell of tears. "I won't let it be!"

"What?" Richard said, frowning curiously. "Oh. No. That's not my blood. Silly chap went and shot himself in the tumble. This is why I don't approve of guns, they are quite frightful things."

Ellie shook her head incredulously, then threw her arms around Richard, pulling him in so tight he let out a gasp as she squeezed the air from him.

"Oh," he said, looking up at Georgie who was deathly pale and shaking her head slowly. "Well, I say. I'm not sure that—"

Ellie pulled back, taking both of Richard's cheeks firmly in her hands and staring hard at his awkward face. "Richard. Please. Don't speak!" She pulled him in again, and this time he was silent.

# CHAPTER 22

"WELL you see, again," Richard said, holding his hands up to push back the barrage of praise coming from all around the table, "as I always say, a proper English education equips a fellow for any eventuality. I was schooled from an early age on how to take 'man and ball' as it were. I simply imagined myself on the rugby field at Eton and executed the tackle in a way I like to think would have made my old games master proud."

"You were amazing, Richard," Sarah said, squeezing his arm tightly. "I only wish I had been there to see it."

"Thank you, yes, thank you," Richard said, fiddling self-consciously with his collar. "I just did my best."

"And I'm glad you did," Ellie said, lifting her glass in salute. "I thought I was a gonner for a minute. I don't know what I'd do without you, Richard, after pulling me from the swamp that's the second time now you've saved my life."

"Well," Richard said with a soft smile, "I suppose it's only fair, you have saved my life too."

Ellie shook her head. "I don't think Jim Turnbull would ever actually have shot you, even if I hadn't turned up that day."

Richard hesitated for a second, then shook his head. "Oh, yes. Jim, I'd forgotten about that. Yes, I should thank you for that too."

Ellie stared at Richard, trying to read his expression. "I thought that's what you were—"

"Oh, I absolutely adore this!" Sarah called out, clapping in time to the lively beat the band had just struck up. "The Charleston! It's the very latest thing." She stood to direct her clapping at the band: Clay, Amos, Ben and Tommy – together for one last night before they returned to America, a special guest appearance at the Starlight Club.

Richard bobbed his head in time to the music, drawing a smile from Ellie and a pair of very raised eyebrows from Georgie. "Yes, it does have rather a catchy beat," he said.

"Come on Dickie," Sarah beamed, grabbing his hand. "It's time to take to the dancefloor."

"Another dance?" Georgie said, a cheeky grin on her face. "Are you sure, Richard? People will talk."

"Let them," Richard said, pulling his shirt sleeves straight. "I have learned to be spontaneous!"

Richard stood sharply, Ellie smiling incredulously at his confident manner in snapping his fingers along to the music.

"Glad you listened to me," Ellie said, "now go out and—"

Richard put his hand out to Ellie. "Miss Eleanor Blaine, I should be delighted if you would dance the Charleston with me."

Ellie shot a glance at Sarah, whose face was rapidly turning the same purple as her expensive-looking silk dress. "I think Sarah wanted—"

"To blazes with what she wants, I wish to dance with you," Richard said. "And I shan't take no for an answer."

Sarah let out a sharp gasp, as Georgie instinctively ducked her head anticipating at the very least a swift and expensive shower of Krug champagne from the glass she was holding. Instead, close-lipped and fuming, Sarah picked up her bag and stormed away from the table to retrieve her coat.

"Richard," Ellie said, lightly scolding him. "That wasn't very gentlemanly, you should have asked—"

"Stuff and nonsense," Richard said. "To be perfectly honest, Sarah is a very handsome woman, but she has done nothing but grill me about my famous patients, or else complain that our restaurant was not expensive enough nor my suit sufficiently tailored, the whole time I have spent with her. She may be a beauty, but she's also a crashing bore, and terribly difficult to put off. Now, shall we dance, or shan't we?"

Richard put out his arm, and Ellie took it with a shrug towards Georgie, who offered a wink and a raised glass in return, and they stepped out onto the dance floor just as the band picked the beat up to an even faster tempo.

Ellie smiled broadly as Richard began to move his long legs in a way that, while perfectly co-ordinated, didn't really match up to any dance moves she'd seen before. "Nice dancing style," she said, half-laughing.

"Thank you," Richard said, returning the smile. "I believe I have a little facility in the terpsichorean arts."

Ellie pulled a face. "I'm sure you do," she said. "And you can dance too!"

As they danced closer to the stage, Clay leaned forward towards them, holding his bass so the neck was almost on the boards, but still keeping a perfect rhythm going. He nodded to the two of them. "Hey, there's some cool moves you got there, your lordship. Real swinging," he said with a grin.

Richard looked at him and nodded a polite thank-you. "That's very kind. Another important part of a gentleman's education is to become familiar with the act of co-ordinating one's movement in time to a set tempo. One never knows when one might be called upon, in matters of diplomacy, to perform an unfamiliar dance at a ball or social gathering."

Clay stared incredulously at Richard for a moment, then shook his head. "Man, that is the squarest thing that has ever been said in any jazz club anywhere in this wide world. But, hey, the square can dance!"

Clay jumped up, laughing and still shaking his head, then nodded to Ben to pick up the tempo again, as the song span up to a crescendo, ending with a crash of drums and loud cheers from all around the club.

Ellie let out a long breath, looking at Richard as she took hold of his hands. "Well, that was a little fast, even for me. Thanks Richard, you certainly put a smile on my face after a pretty tough week."

"My pleasure, as always," Richard said, dropping his head in acknowledgement.

"You see," Ellie said. "I told you being spontaneous was fun. You're the smartest man I know, Richard, but sometimes I think you spend too much time thinking. Isn't it more fun not to worry about appearances and just let yourself go? Sometimes you have to stop listening to your head and just listen to your heart."

"You are absolutely right," Richard said. "And that is exactly what I shall do."

"Good!" Ellie said. "Because when–"

The words had barely left her mouth when they were stopped by the force of Richard's lips as he pulled her in to a tight hold to kiss her firmly. She pulled back instinctively, putting her arms up between the two of them to push him back and away. Richard looked at her, his face still for the briefest second, before collapsing into an expression of unrestrained embarrassment, flushed hot, eyes closed in realisation.

"Oh, Good Lord, I am so sorry!" he said, clasping his hand to his mouth. "What have I done?"

Ellie shook herself down, blowing a heavy breath through pursed lips. "Richard! I wasn't saying... I didn't mean—"

"No," Richard said, shaking his head forcefully. "No, of course you didn't. I have been an absolute buffoon. And I'm rather afraid I have made a complete fool of myself. Please accept my deepest apologies for my totally unwarranted and inexcusable behaviour, and please... I should leave now."

Richard turned sharply, his face glowing with shame, and strode quickly across the crowded dancefloor, not even stopping to apologise to a man he accidentally walked into as he went.

Ellie stood still for a moment on the dancefloor, watching him disappear. She shook her head, then stepped up onto the lower step of the stage to call out after him. "Richard, wait. It doesn't matter. It was just a misunderstanding, we can forget about it. I've forgotten already. Richard, please!"

He turned out of the club door, not hesitating nor looking back, and Ellie started to move through the crowd in his direction. As she stepped up the brief flight up from the dancefloor Georgie stepped out in front of her, blocking her way with her arm.

"Ellie, dear thing," she said, shaking her head sadly. "Let him go. It won't do to try to talk to him now, he'll be quite mortified. But it's our dear Richard, you know how he is. Probably had one or two champagnes too many, and got his blood stirred up, what with all the guns and knives and drama and whatnot. He'll be thoroughly ashamed of himself, probably hide away in one of his fine houses for a week or two, then he'll put his stiff upper lip back on again and he'll be right back to being the old Richard before you know it, don't you worry."

"Yes," Ellie said, her face falling. "I guess you're right. He'll be right back to the old Richard."

\* \* \*

"You ok, Ellie? You're not saying much?"

Clay leaned over the table to try to catch Ellie's eye, as she stared seemingly into space, unconsciously swirling the little of her champagne that was left in the glass. She snapped back into the room at his voice.

"What? Oh, yes. I'm fine, just listening to the music," she said.

The impromptu jazz band had finished their set, and now it was the turn of the Starlight Club's house band to serenade the few remaining customers who had stayed after midnight to listen, dance and drink into the early hours of the morning.

Clay nodded at the band. "Didn't think this was your kind of music?" he said.

"No?" Ellie said. "Not usually, but I'm enjoying it. They're pretty good."

Clay shrugged. "Well, they ain't got much swing, but I guess its alright, for this time of night."

Ellie gave a weak smile. "You'll be tired for your trip tomorrow," she said. "I think your train leaves in about five hours now."

"You tryin' to get rid of me?" Clay said with a mischievous smile.

Ellie laughed. "No, just thinking about home," she said. "I suspect you'll be glad to get back?"

"Sure will," Clay said.

"What will you do? Now the band is finished."

"Hey," Clay said, "every door that closes is another one that opens, right?. Me and Amos, we're putting a little something together. We reckon on 'The Amos Jackson Swing Sensations!' What do you think?"

Ellie nodded. "Yep, I like it. It's a good name."

"It is," Clay said, lifting a glass and glancing over to where his friend sat talking with Tommy and Ben at a corner table. "It's a very good name." He took a sip from his glass, then turned back to Ellie. "You thinking of going back yourself?"

Ellie shrugged. "I'm not sure," she said. "Maybe."

"Well, if you do, you be sure to come and look us up. Come to a show. Hey – maybe see us when we're playing Indiana. I'd sure like to see you, if you did."

Ellie smiled more genuinely now. "If I do, of course I will. I would like that as well."

Clay hesitated for a moment, as if weighing up his words. "Say, that was quite the scene on the dancefloor earlier," he said cautiously. "Everything cool with you and Richard?"

Ellie held up her hand, batting away the question. "Oh that? That was nothing. Really."

"Somethingest looking nothing I've seen in a while," he said, with a knowing smile.

"Honestly," Ellie said, "it really was nothing. Absolutely nothing at all. Would you like to dance?" She stood up as the band started up another number, a slow refrain carried on clarinet over a steady, gentle beat.

Clay smiled, putting out his hand for her to take. "Sure, I'd love to."

As she stepped onto the dance floor, she realised she knew the tune, played a little differently than she had heard it before, but unmistakable nonetheless: All By Myself, the same sad, sweet melody, full of melancholy and longing.

She put her arm to Clay's shoulder as he held her waist and turned her slowly on the dancefloor. "You like this song?" he said.

"Yes," Ellie said, nodding slightly to herself. "Yes, I do. Do you?"

"Well, its sweet enough," he said. "But I'm not sure it's my kind of thing, least not the way these cats are playing it. I like music with swing, I'm not sure you have swing in England. I guess I prefer the pace of life back home. Don't you miss it?"

Ellie shrugged. "I suppose. I think about it a lot. But there's something here in England all the same." She pulled back a little, still with her arm on Clay's shoulder. "I mean, it's a bit like this song really. Yes, its a bit old-fashioned, a little slow, not really what I thought I would like. But it's got something to it, if you give it time. I don't know what it is, just something; it just kind of finds a way to connect with you. To your soul. Do you know what I mean?"

Clay let out a heavy, affectionate laugh. "Oh yeah," he said, "I know exactly what you mean."

Ellie glared at him, his face set in a broad, mischievous grin. "Parry Clayton! What are laughing at?"

Clay shook his head gently. "I'm laughing at nothing, Miss Ellie. Absolutely nothing at all."

Ellie stared through narrowed eyes at Clay for a second. Then she closed them and put her head on his shoulder as they turned around the dancefloor. She let the soft, familiar music wash over her, wrap her in the warmth of its melody, and she smiled.

*THE CAT FROM NOWHERE*

*ELLIE BLAINE 1920s MYSTERIES*

# ELLIE BLAINE 1920s MYSTERIES

# ABOUT THE AUTHOR

EM Bolton is the pen name of a husband and wife writing team from the English Cotswolds. He's an historical fiction author and award-winning journalist, she helps disadvantaged children to learn through interaction with nature, when she's not plotting diabolical ways to bump off an assortment of historical characters. They are ably assisted by their old – and very high-maintenance – cat, Snowpea.

Made in the USA
Las Vegas, NV
31 March 2024

88011684R00146